TOMORROW THE VICTORY

TOMORROW
THE VICTORY

John Fraser

AESOP Modern Fiction
Oxford

AESOP Modern Fiction
An imprint of AESOP Publications
Martin Noble Editorial / AESOP
28a Abberbury Road, Oxford OX4 4ES, UK
www.aesopbooks.com

www.johnfraserfiction.com

A catalogue record of this book is
available from the British Library.

First paperback edition 2020

ISBN: 978-1-910301-50-0

Contents

1

SOPHIE

'MOTHER SAID "brush your teeth or they'll fall out" – and I didn't. See! – they're all there, waiting!' and the ancient shows a row of stumps, black and brown. Rambles off.

'He won't talk to us about the revolution', Mack says. 'It's still his, the one he fought for. It's done, won, over, complete – achieved. It's true – some got rich, some left. They built a school, so, all the kids will emigrate.'

'It's you,' she says. 'He'll talk. You don't want to hear. You're building something big to house yourself, and he's a topos. A brick. If you spoke together, you might see how you are wrong. You won't. You've collected him. He's your actor, with your script. You juggle with parts of him – indent, indenture, you say: teeth! all body parts working for us under contract, semi-slaves, whipped and ground, escaping, crumbling down – he's fixed in your chemical, your words, not his. His mother meant – act now, enjoy later. Is that enjoyment? What he has?'

'I'm right, though,' he says. 'He made it, his revolution. No going back, he's stuck with what he is.'

'You've found another stereotype,' she says. 'There's no politics, no philosophy here. Maybe there's theology. I think for you, it's all fresco.'

'Think for him,' he says. 'The fighter. There was light. Then it became time. They say time's more problematic – you measure it all the time, differently, it's slippery. There's a whole closetful of lengths of string ... a length for waiting, breeding, parting, invading, resisting, exiting. Each one – a different measure, thick or thin.'

'How long is our string?' she asks. 'Us two?'

'It's a metaphor,' he says. 'Not history.'

'I'm not into history,' she says. 'I like to know, is all.'

'I think always of your terrible life,' he says. 'Cover it with superficiality like you do – and it's always terrible. Corporations, banks, state, politicos – killers and thieves.'

'Yours is empty,' she says.

'It's the terrible that concerns me,' he says. 'I know because I've not been involved in awful things, it doesn't mean my life, a life, is good. Or touches goodness.'

'There's more complication than you know,' she says. 'You could even rescue me.'

'There's no rescue,' he says. 'You are you. If I rescue you, it's you. Just say your life out loud – it's evident. Everyone would know – a foulness.'

*

'We're on the leading edge of time,' he says. 'All of us who can speak and have a pulse, all on the same plane. Look down – are they building, or dismantling? All grey and ochre – smoky fires of halms, and fires of homes. Here comes the future ... and there it goes, a perfect past! Has someone been here before? What did they make of it? You can't do much with time ... roast it, carve it? It's not on.'

'I'm holding tight,' she says. 'I feel the wind tug at my hair, I need some other bodies round me, it's so cold!'

'Everybody's holding on,' he says. 'Those that aren't, aren't there.'

'Your old terrorist,' she says. 'Harmless and poor.'

'He didn't look so poor,' he says. 'Behind the mound – those goats.'

'Terrorists have changed,' she says. 'Not poor. Young and well-read.'

'I don't know if he could read,' he says. 'It's always a surprise, when old people say they can.'

'There's not many now who fight,' she says. 'You see it on the news, because there's always less. The real stuff's about wind and water, and this heat – not guys with guns and pistols.'

'If there's not people who suffer, it doesn't stick, it doesn't count,' he says.

'That's cinema,' she says. 'That's where you see people suffering. On film. Then where you watch, a whole audience of sufferers. In the beginning, someone holds the camera, someone else does the sound, and then there's someone else who organises.'

Then there's actors, who try to be as real as possible. They offer up themselves, they suffer. You don't, my dear, you don't suffer. It's not our life that's empty, it is you,' she says.

'You don't want to understand,' he says, 'The politics.'

'Yes,' she says. 'It's always something else from what you see. The hunt. Our side.'

★

They drive along an earthy road. On and on, grass and yellow soil, held in by cloudy horizon – something not right, no signs and distances. Then – here it is: a bar, silver and crystal, usual boys nicking loose stuff, begging for more...

'This must be it,' he says. 'There's no more road.'

Around, it's all a dump. You'd climb a rock, then there are sets of cement steps, steep, up under the vault of rock, and at the top – not a door, a slab of iron.

They don't climb up. There is a smell of glue, a quantity – 'That's it?' he asks.

'It says it's worth the visit: once a holy site,' she says.

She's silent. It's a row, an argument, heads turned away, he talks, says what you say, she's silent, walks a step or two in front.

'I'll take you back,' he says. 'Then you can leave.'

'I know that smell,' she says. 'It isn't glue. At least it was a holy site.'

*

'Time for a retreat...' From what? 'Time for a break...' Of what?

The cell has a wheel in the door. 'Chakra,' he remembers.

The first morning, a monkey jumps through the skylight, takes the food left in the wheel.

'You should be quicker,' says the head, the chief monk.

There's no more food that day. You can't go out.

Next day, the monkey takes the food and bites him.

'Maybe you should eat the monkey,' says the monk.

Next day, it's the same: 'You should make a pact,' the monk says. 'Of course, monkeys don't.'

He's too weak to fight the monkey next day. 'One of you should leave before it's too late,' says the monk. 'But the monkey lives here.'

It costs, getting out.

The break has worked.

★

'Harder!' says his friend, Paco. 'Make it harder, and try harder. Hard things you must turn into style. Be a drag queen, if you can.'

'I've been hard things, till they come easy,' he says. 'I was a poisoner, a trader of slaves. I traded things I wouldn't allow to slide down my throat.'

'God loves the banal,' says Paco, his friend. 'When he lets us die, we're all a packet, all the same – you need to be a doctor to tell the women from the men. You're banal. I'll shake you: sit in my motor, we'll go off for a whirligig.'

Paco's auto – black and silver, the seats inside and out, cages for cocks and leads for bears – here's the Bengali district as they whoosh, up go the flares, the Bengal lights, the tigers, tails lit up like neon bullseyes and there's Bengalis mining antimony; and antinomians – all in white, into the cracked gallery they troop, see how they loll their tongues – three anti-popes abreast, orthodox and not, there go the Persian ladies, untrussed before the fall, white shoulders unexplored, winking from the persiennes, their musky bodies ... coils of black hair, parures of emeralds – 'faster, faster' Paco shouts – 'hold tight, dear Gottlieb, for the love of gods' – here the soil's red, bees burrow, rings grey and black the centipedes, down in the rift the abyss, up on the scree – the wild: the black, the white, a stretch of windows all askew, 'quick, Gottlieb, have some sex, you climb up on the sill, strip off, put your tiny bee sting in the rubber people, see them deflate and so do you, one prick, you die...' Paco accelerates, there's the immortal Engels on the prom, his beautiful mistresses sucking him down, back in the hole – his natural remedies in jars and demijohns, bales of elder loaded on the Snark, up the gangplanks go green boys, spring eternal from chrome plating, their jaws burned off by phosphorus...

There's a hunting green ... a uniform; why, it's Baffone, what a growth! no decent Georgian without a pair of bushy ones – no poncy wax on him, invented by the terrorists, their sky-blue togs up to the scaffold, what a bore, nonsmokers all, the kerbs here all lit up in glaze and glitter – no overbordering, no incursions and no madrasas nodding off, the tramtracks lined with sleepers in their greasy bags, lights, more lights, the trolleys flush them out, and not a word...

'Enough, enough, Paco,' shouts the miscalled Gottlieb, 'I'm blown through like a tube, not loved by gods, not loving them, not Gottlieb now... I am restored! The happy devil, smith of Ghent, the renegading Gabriel sounding his crumpled horn, Ichabod – now, born again, your old friend Mack appears...'

The motor slows and chokes...

'Well,' says Paco, 'that's my advice. I've shown you almost everything. People, city. Another time, we'll look into my stone mine. That's all the rest – time, strata, gaze. You're back on track, old friend, that's the scene, that's all there is round here, you've seen it all, the right speed, right revolutions, right terror if you will, city of corpuscles, red white and green...'

'You're right, Paco,' Mack says. 'I can handle it. You're right – the speed. You have to get it right, and – turn the hard parts into style.'

'Yes,' says Paco. 'That way you're immortal, so long as you can keep it up.'

'When I was with Sophie, I drove too slow,' says Mack. 'That's why she went so silent.'

'Yes,' Paco says. 'Remember those centipedes. With all those legs, they don't go so far. It starts with rocks. You must be one. It ends as rocks. You'll be long gone. You might choose a colour, though. The amethysts...'

'Fuck it!' Mack thinks. 'How come Paco sees so deep? And has a classy auto too!'

'Time,' Paco says, 'is a trampoline. You flex your knees, mind your head against those beams, and – one at a time! Up and up! You bounce! It's up and up to you, you could go for ever.'

They sit under the lime trees with their bocks. There's a smell of jasmine and coffee. Coffee – 'Slavery,' says Paco. 'The written contract, indenture, is the local form. One of the most binding – there's no informal getout, and no ritual. Hereditary, essential to the host. You're branded – not on the cheek, but on the cheeks, where you sit, discharging what's needed for your keep, your salutations to the boss. Bosses? Branded through and through, dear Mack, old friend...'

'My old terrorist, the revolutionary – he escaped that, as he'd fought to do, but he had goats...' says Mack. 'No indenture, no room for dentures... Goats...'

'It's a limitation,' Paco accepts. 'Every explorer went for man- and woman-power; importing children is the best, of course. Lasting longer, if you give them food. Every conqueror – the same. What say you, of the revolutions? The great con...'

'I hadn't thought,' says Mack. 'I'm looking for a contract. No one wants to buy. There's people moving everywhere, each anxious to show docility...'

'It won't end,' says Paco. 'Unless you get true liberation. I'm working on it, whatever it might be. Perhaps...'

'Perhaps there isn't. Every written thing – it's an indenture on your time, your mind, consent, conviction. Nothing is serious, everything melts, every project rides its wing of time, then falls ... you change your luck, double your hopes, your stake, or, if you don't, there – it's that trickle, running down the drain. There goes your luck...' says Mack.

'Well,' Paco says. 'No regrets. If you were sentimental, you'd have cried when Sophie left. It's an old and fusty thought, mine, to escape the extinction... Given, from our past, hanging from those trees, then the savannah... Successors now – we have invented them, crass metal things that run on batteries and drive our cars. We're on the outs already, thanks to our big brains...' He weeps.

'Don't tell me why I'm wrong,' he says. 'Land, gold – now the truth: the quest for purity... Grass beats soil, brass sounds where gold is leaden. Pure truth? I'll write it down for you – lend me your pen... These bottles – remember when the aces fought above the clouds, drinking, throwing the empties at their foes – grenades and grenadine... And are they still up there? Drink, drink up...'

'I don't fear flying,' says Mack. 'My fear's of falling.'

'How many times do I hear that!' says Paco. 'Fear's fear. What do you want, Mack? I showed you everything there is to see. Maybe not the drunks in doorways – you can imagine those. But you know – half the world is women: they're called that. Every shape, and every wish. You wanted one, just one? Staked it all on just one of them, one could be not here or there, and not with you? That was a bold bet, Mack, no one would counsel it. You could have wanted other things, and gone for them: addiction. A mantra. A hamster in a wheel. If it was a slave you wanted – there's all kinds – some you inherit, some you capture, then you manumit or screw. Some you shackle, some you contract, write an indenture. Revolution – that's big, in the history of slavery, and sometimes you end with goats – you have to cut their throats. Hang them up, by their feet, make their ending really sweet...'

'You're right, Paco,' says Mack. 'You can't take it serious. No one takes risk or vanity serious – except an idiot.'

★

If you don't know very poor people, Paco's place would surprise you. It's not an empty suitcase with nothing in it, it's an empty duffel. Everything there is, is waxed paper, paper, or a plastic bag.

'The car, Paco, is magnificent,' says Mack. 'Take me for another turn around. I know, so long as we are in it, that it's yours.'

Paco borrows, for the gas.

'Take me for a spin, Paco,' says Mack.

The way they'd have known each other, Paco, Mack, is if they'd been together in a war, even on some different sides. The same war, of course, the same places more or less. Same jokes to pump them up.

Paco drives so slow – a throb in five-eight time. 'I want to save some speed,' says Paco. 'Want to right injustice with it, build a hill and then on it – a tent, yes – a tent made of feathers, freely given. See, Mack – the hoopooe and its lover, the nightingale, bedded down. The parliament of birds – that's the best – they'd like to love us, Mack, but we don't hear their counsel.'

'Yes, I see that,' Mack says. 'I really do. How d'you get it out, though?'

'You try to follow them,' Paco says. 'In the melody, the ornament. You'll see – you can't. Listen! There, in the carpet, that drabness – the figure ... that's a thrush...'

'There's so many kinds,' says Mack. 'You can't pick each one out... Some are so high up, it's like the sky is tuned...'

'You needn't follow all at once,' says Paco, weaving the motor though a kind of camp, people in long clothes frying onions – 'You'd be crazy that way.'

They cock their heads. Paco says, 'The complexity brings wonder. And after all, the winged creatures live so spare, on the edge of chance – a freeze, a cat, a stone: and they are no more: one identical is already on the stage... So simple, holding on their wire – and yet ... unsingable. No human can aspire. Every bird an artist, untutored and alone, a genius-machine. Not ever to be accompanied, no warble, no whistle, no glissando and no flutter. It must mean so much – the ornament upon the stark... It defeats us, Mack, our hopes, our future, our rehearsals. A chorus without ever an accord, ensemble. Yet – there is a general principle. A life is spent in repetition which is not repeated ... it's an elaboration, same phrase at different times, for hanging dangers, a self-quotation, a truncation, soliloquy – all tradition and all personal unique...

'Doesn't it infuriate? The trills quite meaningless, the life an end unto itself yet thrown away quite wantonly... the matchless leg that slips, the penetrating wing that dislocates...'

The motor creeps from stick to stone, tremulo to robust: 'You could live in it,' says Mack.

'Oh no,' says Paco. 'There is no convenience. My parents – what would they have thought, seeing me perching in a mobile home... I need...'

'What? What could you need?' asks Mack. 'You've nothing. That shows you need for nothing.'

'Aurora,' says Paco. 'I need room for her.'

'She doesn't live with you,' says Mack.

'She comes by. She has a skin, makes you think of marshmallow. She's fascinated. She thinks I'll end by chopping her, with an axe.'

'It sounds pointless,' says Mack. 'I know about these things.'

'You don't know about things without a point,' says Paco, driving fast, round the rim, the city a candied blob, red orange green, down in the cone ... could have been built up here, instead, it's another city of the blind like Byzance clinging to a waterless shore with Asia sweet and cool a bridge away – using mirrors to catch the sun, at midday it is dark – the mountains – a metaphor for absent muses, maybe a missed appointment with a deity. He who breaks the aerials, nicks the hubcaps, wounds the spare wheel with long yellow fingernails, combustion whistle made by a toad, run over in his gulley by an ignoramus parking to take in the nature; the plump soul's ghost given up as water absolutely pure ... on, on, past those wooden houses rocking on their beds of leathery shitsticks, everything up here ready to fall down to there, ending in a superstore of tumbled stuff stored up in thirty storeys. Not far above go disassembled packages of cranes, each slipstreaming, their eyes closed, brains stacked lofty waiting over Africa...

'You build up high,' says Paco. 'Then you need to put some walls around. Down in the hollow, though, you have never closed the city gates. Let them come, riding waist high in blood, and then they'll need relax, sex and a blessing from our father...'

'Round too many times,' says Mack.

'You're right,' says Paco.

They stand aside as Paco lets the auto slide, bounce to the bottom.

2

AURORA

'IF SHE'S HURT,' Paco says, 'It won't be with an axe. It's hard to change your mind if you're using one of those.'

'I expect she'll wish you still had the motor,' says Mack. 'That was the interesting part.'

'If you've nothing someone can envy,' Paco says. 'It leaves you free not to bother about them.'

'Excuse me,' Mack says, 'That sounds the falsest tritest thing I've heard today.'

'So it may be,' Paco says. 'See if I care.'

His kebab pieces come wrapped. 'Look!' he says, reading off curlicues in the paper. 'Cannibalism – it's the latest thing.'

'It's not you,' says Mack. 'It's true – seeing that beast impaled, we all wonder who it was, what prince – but Paco, you throw things away, hoping that what's left is the kernel, the eye... Flesh has its limits, you know. Nothing you put inside is valuable. Happiness is never within...'

'Of course I know,' says Paco. 'Nothing I take in brings revelation.'

'Throwing away,' says Mack, 'is destruction in the abstract. Suicide. Happiness comes before you count the tablets, load the pistol... It brushes you – its wing, its song ... the nightingale.'

'Aurora,' says Paco, turning to her, she's fascinated by the intellectuality all round... 'Were yours Bulgars?'

'Only a grannie,' Aurora says. 'She explored. She didn't impale – that was before. And that was waste, not food.'

'I'll leave you the kebab,' says Paco. 'And the history.'

'She had a chauffeur,' Aurora plods on. 'And an open tourer. Stuck in the sand outside Mecca.'

'All part of the world we're familiar with,' says Paco.

'What you don't know, you pick up at school,' says Aurora.

'You must have been an inspiration, sitting there in writing lessons,' Mack says, riskily. 'A ripe fruit.'

'Oh,' says Aurora, unfazed. 'I wonder how long they'll have them, schools. It's like listening to Homer. The Homer person knew how it was all going to end – not for a minute did he take me in. There's much simpler ways to knowledge, stories even.'

'For everything,' Paco agrees, 'but the gaps for transgression dwindle...'

'When it's so easy, it becomes unthinkable,' she agrees. She says to Mack,

'What I don't see is – we know where we all come from, and where we end. But Paco – all his detail! How can it be so fascinating? He can't accumulate, he's always a newborn.'

Mack says, 'The past can have a meaning. The future – none. My past has no significance, it's all been arbitrary. The present doesn't interest, because, you're right – the future's all been written down as fantasy. Life's just transit, one thing comes, another must.'

'It isn't that,' Aurora says. 'You can make a story – especially if you've got the cash. But Paco...'

'Paco's a mole,' says Mack, 'blind, frantic – he feels the roots of all the trees, imagines how they stand up there. He'll never see one, anywhere. He burrows. Dark. With his claws he undermines what stands tall above. Maybe it's a desert. He won't know. It all ends in a heap, for all of us, someone else, unthinkable, takes over.'

'But you'd rather be a Paco,' says Aurora.

Mack says, 'You've not been following. I took the care to say. I'm not a detail in his design – that's you. You're like a spirit, the spirit of the tree.'

'Oh,' she says, 'I'm not afraid – no more of him than anyone. We're all afraid, we girls, always, you may have read. Anyway, if I'm a spirit, that's quite secure.'

'No,' says Mack. 'Even if you think a spirit may exist – you fall, fall with the tree. Axe or mole – how would you care? It falls. They always do.'

'Paco lets these weird people use him,' says Aurora. 'Everyone is weird, if you look up at them. The nostrils, specially...'

'Passivity is conscience balm,' says Mack. 'High life, low life – let it all use you, you don't need discriminate. Me, I prefer to drive. Keep to the right – you don't need other rules.'

'There'll be a party,' Aurora says. 'It's not for juveniles – purple Jesus in the aquarium – poor fish! – no, it's serious. For cash. He gives wisdom in return...'

'I lent my last for gas,' says Mack. 'It's too unsafe to go down and suck it out.'

'Maybe the President will come,' Aurora says. 'The room is large. He's used to borrowing the cash. He needs the wisdom too.'

'You should sing, Aurora. Blacks used to sing, then came the whites – they couldn't hold a note, and so their funny chanting made a scene somewhere in between...' says Mack.

'Oh Mack,' Aurora says. 'That's all gone by! When you are President, there's only two tunes you need to know – one you salute, the other tells you "walk".'

'I like the in-between,' Mack goes on. 'Between things genuine, there's no in-between. I don't go for originals. That's why – if the President came – we'd only have a stand-in. There's lots, or else – his time would soon run out! He'd never open things or kill bad guys.'

'Is there an original, then?' asks Aurora, fascinated. 'An ur-president? Or are they all a copy of each other?'

'Well,' Mack says, 'apart from the logistics – being everywhere at the weekends – there is the first, who starts it off. Unlike all the rest. Then there is history, tradition. Precedent. Rough and tumble, rough trade too. How'd you keep one chaste, undamaged, maybe for some years? Paco is fierce with words, intent on where he'd like to travel to – but just suppose he did the deed, and chopped a President. It happened once, and so they realised in future, they'd need look-alikes. The people's will, my dear – is just like yours – a lover goes, another one arrives – looks quite alike, if not identical. With kings, it's all expected – same name, same vices... Sometimes one is duff, delinquent, defective... With Presidents – you must depend on silhouettes. The physical resemblance must remain alike ... a series...'

'Oh well,' Aurora says. 'It's disappointing. One warrior falls – another rises up. You plant a milky tooth. I'd heard a story similar.'

'Of course, he may well come, or she, the guy they televised,' says Mack.

'There's nothing wrong with it,' Aurora says. 'Doubles. What's illegal is trying to find out.'

'Paco has ideas,' says Mack, 'It's that they're impossible without cash from everybody else. He wants us all to have a simpler life – inevitable, if he borrows all we own...'

'Nothing is right or wrong,' Aurora says, 'unless you have a scale outside. But – there's no outside.'

'There's argument,' says Mack. 'Logic. Dialectics, dialogue. That's your outside.'

'No, no,' Aurora says. 'We need criteria – what's good and bad. Not who wins an argument.'

'Talking of doubles,' Paco interrupts. 'It isn't true, none of all that. If anyone is cut, cut with a knife, say – at my party, it doesn't matter who it was – whoever did it takes the blame. So, anyone resembling the President – President they are. Gender's irrelevant. Good and bad – they don't come in: responsibility is the thing, in law. Did you do it? Same with me, my doubles. We are one.'

'It's in your brain,' says Mack. 'The answer. They've done it, with those rats and flies: false memories, the dream relived. The last thing to rely on is your brain, your common sense. Not common, not remotely – someone does the test. That's your "outside", Aurora – there's the philosopher who says – "In the last resort, it's up to you – you do the test..." But – no! Not you ... your brain is perishable, like tripe that's boiled in milk and left outside ... the heat, heat of the day, the flies...'

'There!' says Aurora, hugging Mack and laughing, flicking a button on her blouse and showing off some breast. 'There's your outside. You said it, Mack! Tripe...' She can't stop laughing, and Paco pinches her –

'No one gets hurt,' he says. 'I don't know many people, anyway. There's freaks and people from the street – their life is party, mine's a bore...they have to bring the stuff themselves, if they want to eat and drink.'

'Oh Paco,' says Aurora. 'There's more than eat or drink. There's all the stuff you take to fuck your brain...'

'Everything is test, experiment,' says Paco. 'That's what makes life interesting. What would make it valuable – is if there is a person, or a plan, that evaluates the tests and the experiments, that watches and records ... Otherwise, it's just a waste of time, laboratory unattended, beasts out their cages, larking round...'

'That's awful, Paco,' Aurora says, still giggling. 'We think we are the subject of all the odd chance things we do – but what makes it meaningful is – if we're the object of some project that we don't know what it is or why...'

'Well,' says Mack, 'isn't that the oldest thing! The Spirit, Paco... We give you cash, you disappear. Our loss? We charge it to ...'

'That's it,' says Paco. 'You charge it.'

★

'And so,' says Mack. 'We're amateurs. We always arrive back at the start. It's all familiar – at the heart of everything there's something indescribable that always looks the same.'

'It all goes back to Paco. At least we know him. He's not a mystery, he is everything,' Aurora says.

'Maybe he'll take you with him, Aurora. Or you could follow him – or maybe come with me. I am more laughs, you'll see,' says Mack, not too convinced of any one of these...

Aurora too is not convinced: 'There's first the party, and we'll need security. A band. Maybe security and music both combined, a band of Angels, to watch over everything.'

They stare at each other – each inedible, one feathered, the other – an oily pelt. 'Remember, I'm not big enough to

live in a house,' says Aurora. 'I only fill a room. Houses
have cellars with a drunken family, biffing one another,
reaming their noses with cinnamon sticks, an attic with a
soldier, a helmet skewed upon his head, open flies. Where
do you live, Mack?'

'I don't live anywhere,' says Mack. 'What's living? Your
rich father sends you off to learn to be a shit. He hates
them, shits like he pays you to become...'

'So, your father was rich?' asks Aurora, opening the deep
box she'll put him in, giving it a shake.

'No,' says Mack, 'he had money hidden, but he lived like
a poor shit. It gave him height.'

'That's enough,' Aurora shouts. 'All that old dead stuff!
Leave it for the hard rain, the gardener's rain that turns it
into something else. Marrows and broccoli...'

'You're tough, Aurora,' says Mack. 'You'll roll wherever
you are dropped.'

'I can't wait,' Aurora says. 'When the Arabs get their
country ... I'll be Scheherazade.'

'That's not easy,' Mack says. 'Especially if you don't
know stories. Then there's the fighting. I've seen places
where it's all been settled long ago, and the fighting still
goes on.'

'Don't be a baby, Mack,' Aurora says, laughing. 'It
always goes like that. Keep an eye on the sky, like they say,
and one on the door ... if they knock, it shows they're not
so serious...'

'They wouldn't come for you,' says Mack. 'You're
Aurora! There's nothing they can do to you!'

3

PACO'S PARTY

NO ONE EXPECTED it would be like that. Nothing except talk – it palls. His empty room's up high – out of the window, all who dare, on a lower slope of roof they rush – Aurora first, straddling a rooftree, others sporty in their workclothes, blue, orange, a row of hoopoes, talking of monkeys, King Ludwig, whatever comes to mind...

'I must get rid of them,' says Paco, his face a fever-spot: 'Why did I want this? The monkey theme – I know they take our habits, have a boss, and executions, old guys have all the sex... It's tragic, that it comes to this, of course, the other species copy us, compete to be extinct first...'

'Monkey tales, Paco,' says Mack. 'Everyone has one. Now they'll never go, the blues and oranges – on the roof, a troop, a flock...'

'I'm off,' says Paco. 'I'll re-invent baroque. I'm finishing off those movies – hundreds, Lang, Welles, Visconti... I've German actors too – fierce! "Fuck you!" that's all they know; if they don't understand. I'm the only finisher who doesn't want the fame. I'm what they call "discredited". I finish off, I don't appear.'

'But...' says Mack, as Paco would expect.

'They all end identical,' Paco says. 'That's the secret of great art. No surprises.'

'You'll be back, Paco, soon,' says Mack. 'Remember when they said that being a communist was a moral duty? You went backwards, before all that; you're safe. It's yet to come, everything. I left it all behind, the wake – I'm up on the deck, the prow – it's all behind me – I've no duties left. We've all done everything today, every one of us: we're liberals, free as happenstance will let us, surviving, splayed out in the sun, us happy pigs, lucky on monthly pay. Social as well – all in it for the greater good... Nothing's too wild for us – today as executioners, tomorrow hiding in a hole, bankrupt millionaires, merchants of the nightsoil... Everything is odd, there are no people oddities, we've walked the steppe, the asphalt, the chalcedony, past and future intertwined, a ying and yang embraced and laced together...'

'Exactly so,' says Paco. 'I can do everything, the present hasn't happened yet, – and nothing is of benefit.'

'And has the President come?' asks Mack.

*

'We see it all, Mack,' Paco says. 'We flinch. We're intelligent, our eyes are sharp, but even so – we're brave. We step out, as if there's solid stuff beneath us. We leave our tracks, I'm sure.'

'Making movies – I'm so pleased,' says Mack. 'I count on you, that you're kept safe.'

'Not so sure,' says Paco. 'I've written out the end. Each one – ends with a battle, with a fight.'

'Oh no,' says Mack, 'maybe a year ago, people hoped for that. This year...'

'You're wrong,' says Paco. 'You think they've seen the battles on a screen, and so turned pacifist. Not so. They want a resolution – victory, or else defeat: chained, humiliated for being weak, the few survivors trafficked off...'

'Every unfinished movie, ending so?' asks Mack.

'Yes,' Paco says. 'People want it, I'm the director. That's how it all ends. That's what they always want. Perpetual birdsong.'

Most are perching on the roof below – someone, yes, might it even be Aurora? – starts reciting. *Poésie concrète.* The sounds come faintly through the glass, Mack feels the intensity ... joy, misery. Everything is broken, everything is recognisable as it lies in shards ... everything is song and sound. It is the nightingale! – the wise counsel, suffering and patience... Who taught the nightingale to sing? Mack wonders, and tells it: all poetry's a lie, only song and sound are true ... the bulbul sings till dawn ... it is the dawn...

'Where's the beat?' he hears a shout...

There's a drummer, there was no band. No Angels, no security. But – this guy's excellent. He puts a heartbeat underneath Aurora's shouts.

Paco leaves, his exit covered by the noise of battered skins.

The high voice, driven on, the pulse, 'stompf ... ugle ...' Can you improve on the original? Is it the same this time? For sure, percussion helps. People are put to death for less, much less, Mack thinks.

*

'That was fun,' Aurora says, tapping to be let in through the window, shouting as it stays closed. 'Don't you have wheels, Mack? Trolling round town with them beneath your backside? Without them, you have to leave, it seems. Paco's gone to Cinecittà to finish off the movies, so we can leave when the last sequence starts, before the end that everybody knows. That way everything will always be immortal, us too, no doubt. What a genius! Paco's the wisest!'

'I enjoyed the poem,' says Mack primly.

'Always different,' Aurora says. 'That's the best kind of poetry. Sounds the way you hear it. Fits the mood. This time no one fell off the roof. Those dumb hoopoes!' And they laugh.

'Of course,' she says, 'When Paco's done the endings – that really is the end. Cinema is finished off. Leaves celebs and millionaires. What next?'

'I always ask you – "come with me",' says Mack. 'There's always an Aurora – and it always sours, it never works. We find our holy site, our terrorist, our hope, our longing... We climb the stairs – there's the iron door. That smell, industrial, of excrement. We quarrel and we split...'

'For you,' Aurora says, 'it never ends. Your ship sails on, and every port is closed. Don't listen to the mermaids, offering love – they guide you on the rocks... You think – it ought to end. A satisfied sleep, someone beside you on the bed. And – you're done. Finished, Mack! The bulbul lives only for its song, it's dark, but who cares? – you don't have a score to read. The others – with those gruesome nestlings – repetition, Mack! No Plato's chemist's shop. No choice between intoxication and cure. There's hawks and rats instead... Fear, anxiety, that's your life you might pass on... There's nets on Egypt's shore, guns in Calabria... No, Mack, sing! If you can't sing, then hop!'

'Migrating,' Mack says. 'It's all neurons and magnets.'

'No, Mack,' Aurora says. 'It's your bones! Forget them!
No bone saw dawn or dusk. Leave them, the place
unmarked. A scrambled pile – those crane-fly legs, the
spider monkey's arms ... the cranium – full stop, alembic
spout downturned – all you know reduced to time and
fashion, and the question – "Where should I leave my
bones?" Forget them, Mack! Some beast will chew on them
– and good for her! You're done with them, and all the trips
they made.'

★

Aurora's flame against the dawn, all rose and gold – but
then – oh no! – a tempest swells above the roof. The others
hunker down, like gall-nuts, like barnacles closed against
the tide – but Aurora's pressed against the glass. 'Open the
fucking window, Mack,' she shouts, she's splayed against it,
fingers and satin sleeves like seagull's wings, white struts –
the flying aces and their mechanisms washed up, feather
and bone combined. 'Open...' Aurora screams...

Mack can do nothing. 'Back off, Aurora – in the
beginning, all glass was liquid, like pure cane syrup ... a test
push against, then you're through...' But no – maybe those
drapes, the design, maybe a hex...? It's solid, a desert.

'The storm's a test,' shouts Mack. 'The window's
nailed...'

'It can't be so,' Aurora shouts. 'We all came out... I sang
my song, and now. My nest, Mack! – let me back in... I
forgot to mention, how I loved poor Paco, unrequited,
naturally, my story – not a word, a twist can change: no
other character, poor Mack, can enter in... You should have
known – those cans of movie – you can't change a frame,
Paco'll only add the predetermined end...'

'The storm will pass, Aurora, most birds survive, rebuild the nest,' says Mack. 'Adventures with you – they're quite impossible unless they fit the storyline and Paco's final cut...'

She's flat against the glass. Mack doesn't try to lift the pane, the frame. The water's washed it clean, the glass – so clean like never was – all of hers exposed, a pinkish frosted bride, not quite deflowered, but all the petals blasted off ... the bulbul silenced, what's to do, but sing the same song over, over and over, an everlasting gala tour...

'There!' says Mack. 'The wind has passed. Go help the rest...'

He's given up. The memory, regret, relief – all over, finished. Time to leave.

FOREIGN RELATIONS – THE COMMITTEE ROOM

'Monogamy. You're the expert, Mack,' the head guy says. 'A wife, a mistress. That requires no counting, but two wives, at the same time – it's an insult.'

'I was there,' says Mack. 'Am I an expert? The place ... discussing its destiny ... we're the gods! That time was, for me, another monogamy.'

'The maths is plain,' the guy, the Chair, says. 'There's many times more women than there's men. That must be so. Where it's the reverse, I expect there's polyandry. That would suit me fine.'

'Is this the highest place where we discuss what's to become of them?' asks Mack.

'Don't worry,' says the guy. 'This is the lowest. We have experts, who've been there. What we think goes up the line.

In the end, it's interests decides: geography and mines. Mostly they look at atlases.'

'I was worried,' Mack says. 'We're so flighty. People there – they're determined, not like us. They eat those goats. They don't know tofu – they're way back.'

'They're slack,' says an expert. 'Don't keep the law. I'd say they're heteros ... heterodox.'

'Some keep the law,' says a colleague. 'But it's a different law.'

'What we need,' a prof says, 'is missionaries of modernity. Of postmodernity as well...'

'Do we nurture them, the guys there – or do we let them drift? Where will they end?' asks Mack.

'I say we're for diversity,' says the Chair. 'Do we protect it? That sounds an oxymoron. Do we simplify? Create diversity or let it flower?'

'I think I should leave,' says Mack. 'I don't understand all this.'

There's many of them, sat in a long room, each with a tessera, jostling to place it in the soft cement, to make a picture recognisable, the Pan ... something, Panto? *crator*, maybe just Pan, or a slow pan, scholarly, from goats to local bosses...

'Come on guys,' the Chairman shouts. 'How do we engage with them, our sisters, brothers, how may things pan out, our interest, philosophy, how will it impact...?'

It is time to say, 'Remember how they made the revolution...' how they see the world we see... Mack's intimidated, doesn't speak.

★

'I saw you nearly drown,' says Fulvio, who'd sat beside Mack in the long high room. 'Don't be afraid. The killing's done much higher up the line. There's presents too, and licences for pills. There's even true belief – but we advise, don't need believe in anything at all. You'll like the fee. Someone must have recommended you. You'll rise from expert in one place to regional... a continent awaits. They ask you back; before you go, you find out something you can say. That's how it is, the species struggles on. You must have read, the heat, the thirst ... we're in the last, the final, the decisive fight... Poor feisty people, with their tribal ways, their powerful friends – what a useless mess...'

'I didn't know how things go on,' says Mack. 'All us strategists...! Of course, I'm quite a fox...'

'I hope that's just a metaphor,' says Fulvio. 'Foxes are on their outs. Speed and greed – they're not enough. There's mirrors, and there's windows, Mack. Mirrors show that whatever you might want to see – it just reflects yourself, your prettiness, your true beliefs, your physiognomy. The windows – true, they are a pond of glass, where everything there is beneath, within, is changed, transmogrified, and doubled up. You see, and you are seen – but there's a barrier, infrangible meniscus – they can't get at you, they're on the other side: and you don't see yourself. They're different kinds of barrier, Mack – we live in mirrors, we pretend we can be windows...'

'Fulvio!' says Mack. 'I fear them both, both sides.'

'Everyone's involved somewhere,' says Fulvio. 'You can't pretend that what you see's a toybox, yours alone. Stare at the mirror – or protect yourself: seal up the window, Mack. Forget yourself, but don't be seen. That is how it is – be very very prudent, take the fee. Don't think of sacrifice – it only means you slough your wings, leap in among the hopeless, souls for sale, dear Mack...'

'It sounds quite *facho* – at least, well, evolutionary,' says Mack.

'Oh, everybody does it, all the time. Those meetings: winners, losers, everyone. All size each other up, the bombers and the bombed, the beggars and the walleted. The species, Mack. That's what's at stake, not just our top spot. Think bees, think ants: the great masters did. Order, organisation: everyone's essential only if they're fulfilled, work at their best. Perfection is the goal, dear Mack,' says Fulvio: 'Perfection, to gain a little time, survive another winter...'

'Sophie must have dropped my name,' says Mack.

'Wild pig sandwiches!' shouts Fulvio. 'We'll stop off here. My favourite!'

★

'Survival,' says Mack. 'That's the theme. But so many suicides...'

'The martyrs, revolutionaries,' says Fulvio. 'Take them into account. Holy men and dupes ... all are on the roundabout.'

'Those boars eat all kinds of crap,' says Mack.

'That gives the flavour, and the fat – it kills us, but it makes the taste,' says Fulvio.

'You were in the Party, Fulvio?' Mack asks.

'That's all done,' says Fulvio.

The sandwiches are excellent. No metaphors. Wild pigs, the martyrs – take them as they come, thinks Mack. *Davai, davai,* thrust from the thighs, backs curved – keep the barges moving...

*

'We're dealt the lowest cards,' says Fulvio, when they are full. 'But we still play the game. We know what places distant, strange, are like. The guys up there, our bosses – they don't care. What they think is perfect – is simpler, stark. But for sure, they're stuck up there. For you, it's all pollution. For me – purification. A battle of the angels for both of us.'

'Countries,' says Mack, 'are nets. They surround the poor fish, deliver them to suffocate and be coshed by bosses they have had to trust...'

'Countries are a refuge,' says Fulvio, 'where you can be with people, some of them – who look and talk like you.'

'Some are palaces with peacocks – you may get to shovel up the plumes and husks. Some are rows of coffin cells, where every day's the same, the smell's the same, the sun is black,' says Mack.

'Be glad each one is different, and you are different in each,' says Fulvio. He belches, eloquent, a wind the wild pigs may have turned their faces to. 'Don't be boring, Mack,' he says.

Mack persists, 'These conflicts everlasting – they're not singular: they're strings of exploding sausages, hung from a cellar roof to dry. People with cellars take themselves so seriously...'

'It's indigestion, Mack,' says Fulvio. 'The swinging fist is always ready where you have us human guys: how'd you expect a troop of monkeys to get organised, squared off, a platoon, sloping arms and forming fours? It's all unnatural, of course. Nature's always there. There's a solution, Mack, to everything: nothing's ever solved. Accept it, Mack. Solutions – you'll only find them in mathematics.'

Fulvio throws up his snack.

'You want to find a person that'll listen to your wails,' he says. 'You think it ought to be a woman – sex and discourse, how convenient. It needn't be a female – it could be me, your comrade in adventures. But – too bad! I don't want it. Distance, Mack!'

'Too rich,' says Mack. 'Those pigs – how they love their little families! Inside, I've given up the flesh, but the temptation stays...'

'It's worse for me, says Fulvio. 'They say "wild pig" – let's hope it isn't pork. For me, it is forbidden, somewhere between transgression and a sin.'

Maybe he'll change his mind, Mack thinks, and want to cleave to me, depend, be intimate. A pal! How terrible, the thought!

*

Mack tells Sylvia, 'I used to live in the US. They went on shooting, after one of their wars. It was like they were all china dolls, and one of them stepped out of line and shot the rest.'

'I thought Mack was American,' says Sylvia. 'That name. The whites cut down on syllables.' She too comes from that long room where they give advice about some other countries. She's elderly, not distinguished physically, but she's smart, she must be, surviving, listened to, for years.

'They don't know about anywhere else but where they are,' Mack persists. 'And people come home from nowhere with dreams so terrible they can't imagine anyone living on, surviving. I was just about the only one to notice, to be alarmed... I lived there, I didn't become it.'

'There's something you can take for that,' says Sylvia. 'Camomile? Valerian? Or are those poisons?'

'When it snows here,' Mack says, 'I put on woollen socks and go up to the refuge – there's ice water and bunk beds. You celebrate a passing of a year: there is polenta, and you give out more socks and stuff to homeless kids. If you don't feel better for it, you don't feel worse, except the cold, and the polenta – it gums you up for weeks.'

'I'd love the address,' says Sylvia.

'It's all voluntary, Sylvia. You do it all yourself,' says Mack. 'The mountain's ice – you can't go down, you'd break your skull, just like an egg. You must go to the services, but you don't need sing – they couldn't make you, anyway. You pray it will be transformed, and done with. You too.'

'I know about the peoples we discuss,' says Sylvia, going red. 'My husband was an officer, sweet as a mulberry. They boiled him. Savages.' She stares ahead. 'They called it revolution.'

'When you boil lobsters,' Mack soothes her. 'They don't scream – it's the process. Air escapes. They hardly ever do.'

'Well,' Sylvia says, 'that's comforting. Mack – you are a humanist. We need your kind – the rest of us is secular.'

'Oh well,' says Mack, desists. He's what you cannot be, a bit of everything.

'Everyone,' says Sylvia. 'Must get their just desserts. Even if you don't make the sign, Mack, wait, and they will come. Sweet or sour.'

'Yes,' says Mack. 'It's like a restaurant – like in Moscow, where they kept imperial menus – roast golden pheasant, broiled sturgeons – you waited, hunger passed – then it might be hamburgers... No one waited for desserts.'

'I wonder if you're up to it,' says Sylvia. 'Any of it.'

'I'd like to see Aurora,' Mack says. 'It's like waiting to see Fantomas... Winged things creeping up the walls, lurking in those intermediate spaces.'

'The city's small,' says Sylvia, put out. 'You might see anyone, many more times.'

'We've seen where we will end,' says Mack. 'It's fun, us being rich and able to dipose of other people's destinies – but we've seen the pictures. In thick lines, waiting to be bussed into even more troubled places, for our religion, or for having none. After religion – does truth come?'

'You haven't understood,' says Sylvia. 'We talk to save ourselves, not the unknown.'

She lives near the roof. She squeezes on the divan, between two tall afghans. Mack has to stand.

'The room smells because they're old,' she says. She too is old. Poor too, it seems. There's spiky metalwork around, a gas ring stood on paper, red spots dropped like sealing wax.

'Dogs,' she says. 'Shoot. Never strangle, when it's time.'

'That's the lesson, then?' says Mack, trying to lighten up.

'That's it,' says Sylvia. 'That's what I learned. I pass things on. Space – it's better filled. Some people live with lots of it. It makes you drift. Best know your boundaries, no emptiness.'

'Big ideas,' says Mack. 'They don't fill little lives. They used to, not long since. Now...' he thinks – there was a gas explosion... and he stares at her black ring, her few treasures yawning, waiting for their chow. 'We say we're in transition, as if we're near the other shore. It isn't so. Transition lasts for ever.'

'Who'd you want to sort it out?' she asks. 'More gentlemen? They weren't so gentle, either. Those ancients with their telescopes, nibs cocked, Purdys loaded, rambling

to the grave. All dead, Mack. Then came the saints and
devils, the terror and the trembling ... what a mess!
Revenge is a driver, Mack, you'll find. Justice. Follow your
instincts, Mack, there's nothing else.'

'I'm not sure I have them,' Mack says, turning to the
door, 'I'm not a gentleman, maybe nothing else.'

'You're wrong about the lobsters,' Sylvia says. 'They
scream. Everybody does.'

*

Paco gives interviews. He's finished all those movies. He's
become famous, to escape criticism. It would take decades
to show those movies in the right places, and have some
people, influential, say they're no good.

*

Mack keeps going back to Sylvia's place. She's the worst
kind – a poor reactionary with airs and arias. 'I'm dying,
Mack,' says Sylvia. 'I want to go down with a bang. Out
from a height, so there'll be no need for autopsy. Maybe
even a surprise – caught in flight and borne up by angels. At
that point I shouldn't care. People don't take to me, but
they're so perverse – they'll want to love and pity me.'

'I wouldn't bet to that,' says Mack. 'I'm not American,
Sylvia, I'm an Azeri, though my parents weren't. There's
much beating in Baku – it might speed your passing, Sylvia,
watching it, making it your show. You mightn't need to go
there: it was a magnificent empire – now it's gone, you
can't ever leave it ... leave them, any of them...'

'Yes, Mack,' says Sylvia. 'I can't stand you. You drip like acid on to stones. You're always in my way – just perverse, you lie, you're ignorant, you're soft.'

'Come off it, Sylvia,' says Mack. 'You know no more about dying than I do. Even though you're closer to it, to nothing...'

'It's not a thing you can be close to, Mack,' says Sylvia, starting to cry. 'Nothing – can't exist.'

'It's on TV,' says Mack. 'We're all in it. There's no money now, so we go in the incinerator, with all our clothes and diaries.'

'We have to give direction to those uncertain countries,' Sylvia says, recomposing herself. 'We don't go on TV.'

★

What would Sylvia leave him? Mack wonders ... an extra skin, a tree's year of standing there.

'I don't have words for what I've seen,' he thinks. 'What did those people think? I'm sure I know, but no words passed. Redbirds in those inverted trees – stumbling up high in the waving roots. Aurora's poetry – sounds like words that push you towards places invisible, provinces of music who've seceded ... terrible slaughters, casualties with arms and legs blown off...'

★

'If we have a child,' Aurora says, 'why not one grown up? Who'd want one that can't see or speak, who chants stupidities? We only live a hundred years. You can't back check. Throw the ball, and chase! And, Mack, you shouldn't leave that group. It might make you feel good, some sense when the meeting's over, of something else to do. They call it moral purpose, that sense? Of course – it unavails: countries aren't young, they don't grow up, nor old. You have no words for what they do and think, and yet you see them, busy, spaced out, staring down a well – you don't communicate, and yet you know, they know ... exactly what it's all about, nothing of where it's all proceeding to...'

'The roof, the window, that was my last sighting ... what then, Aurora?'

'Oh,' she says, 'I expect I fluttered down. You surely can fill in that space? Nothing is blank, no interval! Scratch with a twig, a charcoal finger, write...'

'We love the nightingale' says Mack. 'Her song. But – she is invisible, the song has no words. It's always the same ... or is it similar? We love her dearly, the nightingale, though we don't see her, love the song, even more, when we recall it...'

'You're right,' Aurora says. 'Forget the child. We shouldn't have it. Not I, nor you, nor either.'

*

'What next?' Aurora asks. 'I've done my show. What's left is doing it all better.'

'My parents were Armenian,' Mack says. 'I'm nothing. Everything. All the power there's been is lying in a pool, just plug in and off...! Religion said you were better than the rest. Take the medicine and they do the walks. Whoever stuck it out – was best. If you cared, there was even paradise – but everyone had lost that at the start. It was being better, facing down the world. I still care about being better, but not about being good. Trailing those corpses in their leather sacks behind – that too's best avoided.'

'You're a bigot, Mack,' Aurora says. 'And you'll wear out your shoe.'

'Like Sylvia,' Mack says. 'Hers were red I think.'

'Sylvia has a famous name,' Aurora says. 'She won't say it, nor admit. Her family all ended bad – somewhere out East – not the farthest, but the middle state, one of them, I'm sure. A prelate? A general? All his family, all who bore his name... All who escaped – they ended up like her: nameless, unable to explain...'

'I didn't know' says Mack. 'I have this blindness... I can't see what lies beneath a casual descent, a bitterness, a rage...'

'That's your demon, Mack' Aurora says. 'You're fortunate to have one so understanding, gentle, even. Doors, windows – you never open one: to you, they're walls. You're the exasperating innocent who cannot understand the language that his epic, his destiny, is written in. You may as well not be the hero – you could be the hero's horse except it knows more than you do, understands the orders and endearments, the depth of chasms it must overleap, of rivers it must swim, the force of tempests...'

'Of course a hero's blind,' says Mack. 'Or else he wouldn't play the role. Without a horse, he couldn't make the trek, the metre of its hooves, essential, mile after mile – on foot he'd never reach his end. Singing? That has an end. But – all those couplets – now, who'd persevere? I might drive a Mustang –'

'No,' says Aurora, 'don't be feeble. It's my game, I decide. Horse.'

*

'You can't fiddle with nationalities,' says Fulvio. 'You have to know lots, and avoid lots more, if you want to have one, especially a distant one like yours. And beware – even for an Abkhaz – it's all fading away, never like it was, nor will it be...'

'No,' says Mack. 'You don't need know anything at all. That is the point – about most things you're born with or become – schools and contacts, accidents and doubts. Memoirs – they lie like all the rest of written things.'

'Well,' says Fulvio, 'you can't be what Aurora says you are – you want to be – if you can't recognise the characters in your scene. If you disbelieve, those gods and demons don't exist. There's just jobs: saving people, torturing them. A nullity, dear Mack, a task for bureaucrats, a desk of infinite dimensions. Seek, dig, excavate, Mack – go deep. There is no bottom, naturally, just depths. Don't seek the truth! Something in between. Be reconciled.'

He pulls Mack after him, down dusty alleyways, 'Mmmm,' he says. 'I love this Bangla food – I bet there's pigs – they keep them hidden, as it's easy meat.' He dips his hands in sizzling vats and swirls up gouts of black – nameless battered polyhedrons. 'Taste! This is real life! Pigs? Our brothers... You know, we can transfuse their blood, and transplant trotters too, except that might give offence. Old-time religion – can you imagine that? They are omnivorous, like us...'

'You follow diets, Fulvio,' says Mack. 'You're quite fervent. And yet religion doesn't count...'

'It doesn't count for me,' says Fulvio. 'Leviticus is far too lax, to take one sample: no! There is a promise that there is one diet makes you fly. You know, that when you die, the

soul's released, and flies up to the highest branch, and there
you see them clustering, they chack and chatter, build those
twiggy shrines. But I don't wait until I die. I want to fly,
and maybe do some useful work – those cadavers on
rooftops, waiting for those flighty birds; that Greek guy,
standing with his liver all exposed – it's amateur! I can
release their souls at once, no fee, no casket, and no faff
with vicars, monks and such...'

'That's why you were a pilot, Fulvio?' asks Mack.

'Of course,' says Fulvio, 'Americans have got it right.
Those metal pods you fly, and drop explosive metal pods –
unnecessary repetition, pleonasm in the blue! Those drones
they use are quite in line with all the sacred books – out of
the sky it comes, the summons, and the judgment,
parcelled up and tied together with coordinates upon a
screen. It is divine, dear Mack... But – we must beware. If
we take over from the holy happenstance, make death a
question of some culpability, some guilt – the whole's
traduced! It's goddam puritans at work! Death comes to all
– it's not a matter for judiciary or politics... Down from the
sky, dear Mack, it comes! It's indiscriminate, you can't
pretend only the bad guys die, or are picked out! That's
why we must take care, in our committee – judgment is
given out to everyone, good and bad, young, old, beautiful
or not. Guilt has no place in that.'

'Aurora says I can make history,' says Mack. 'That leaves
her out – she hates it. No relationships – they leave a trace,
like beetles on the glass. I'm not sure what...'

'You're the only one unsure,' says Fulvio. 'That's good.
Syvlia – you've heard her – "Savages" is everyone.
Whatever happens to us all – there is no judgment possible.
Everyone is ignorant, everyone. Whatever has merited their
destiny. That's good as well – the new chief, the boss of

bosses, king of kings – likes a quick fix. She's forgotten what she promised anyway: get it done, she says. So – Sylvia is in. Our recommendation flies swift to the top. You, Mack – you know nothing, so you've an alibi.'

'There must be more that I can give,' says Mack. 'Womens' love for women. The end of landscape. end of otherness, of grass, water, typhoons, smogs and archaeology?'

'We don't have time for that,' says Fulvio. 'We advise about the people. If we all agreed about catastrophe, there'd be no need for a committee. And, Mack, to be a hero, pretending it's for common purposes and not a quest for exoticism – you must hurry up. Time's out, for those like you. You must start young and popular, unless you want to write your book and stack it on high shelves, grow old and dusty...'

'We do what we want,' says Mack. 'We can be criminals.'

'No,' says Fulvio. 'We're the law too. We needn't take things into account, that's all. We can disagree among us – otherwise there'd be no committees: but we reach agreement, or else committees wouldn't be of use.'

'I mean,' says Mack, 'we can advise killing lots, to save the good guys, and to do the right.'

'They have committees too,' says Fulvio. 'Good guys and bad. Fuck off, Mack, don't be childish – forget this cut-out, wall-scribbling stuff. Go on so – and they won't ask you back, pay for your experience.'

'The heroes I know,' says Mack, 'are from my childhood – Zeno, Ulrich ... Serge from Minuit, Obligacion ... Something goes wrong or – there's nothing to go right.'

'I could take you down to where I'm known,' says Fulvio. 'All have an Old Nickname, countries matter there

– not horizontal, equal, laid out on paper, but vertical, like in a heap of mulch. That's where we've learnt to interfere...'

'I know the world is one,' says Mack. 'But – there's many places where I don't belong, can't go. I'm pleased too that all those doors are locked – but ... here, I'm defended, I'm on the winning side, the powerful one – so I feel weak...'

'That's what you wanted, Mack, you and your friends. Weak and voluble. Being in charge of air and fanfares. You're curious about those doors,' says Fulvio. 'What may pop out, and how they're dressed ... you're weak, Mack, not just because you're on the winning side ... it's that you know that once you've won, been winning – what is left is losing, loss. It must come. It's mechanical, it's logical. You win, you lose... What, you ask, have you to lose? Maybe you're losing even now. Defeat – after all, it's certain, and it's not so bad. A spasm. You'll come through, or if you don't, there's not a silence, there's a nothing, nothing left at all: but if you live – what do you do with all your loss?'

'Be like Sylvia, where all's built on loss...' says Mack, 'But I don't want to be like her...'

'No one does,' says Fulvio. 'We'd all like being dear Aurora – no caress from her, no ties. No win, no payout, and no loss.'

'She's beautiful, though,' says Mack. 'Out there, on a roof, ragged against the sky. Who'd want her in a cage?'

'No emotion,' Fulvio says. 'Nothing to be monetised. Simply another person – with no weight at all.'

'How d'you know so much, Fulvio?' Mack asks.

'Oh,' he says, 'I have my Painters. They don't paint – they sell paintings. They're not real paintings – they are reproductions on card. They don't sell many copies – they sell other things. Keys to knowledge you're not supposed to have. They know everything. They set their easels by the palaces, and they hear everything. They come from everywhere, and everybody trusts them.'

'I'm fascinated,' says Mack. 'They show where the lines are – your Painters, criminals. Except – the lines are always hidden. Like shamans, they're the only ones who cross those hidden lines – except we pay them, they let us sing and dance, smoke hash and fall down like we're dead, and yet – they're the only ones who explore, who pass from us to animals, from live to dead...'

'Who says they're criminals?' asks Fulvio angrily. 'They're Painters who don't paint, that's all.'

'I bet they go on missions, expunge people they are ordered to,' says Mack.

'There you have it – orders. Painters don't give or take them. They deal with people exactly like them, that's the other side. There is no crime, none is possible between like people,' says Fulvio. 'There are four kings – always, all equal: unless there's trumps, they're equal, one takes t'other. It's us who make the trumps: it doesn't last – the next hand shifts the power to somewhere else. Then, say, the pot is won, and all the rest have lost... Winner takes all – but all is nothing, because it is the end: there's no game left, no structure, no laughter and no song.'

'Your Painters, Fulvio – they are old hat,' says Mack. 'They watch the powerful and the exiles in the café on the square. It's not like that – there's orders given, and there's information. There's empires, and there's abstraction. There's conjurors and info – the info's everywhere. Pollock over everything. I bet your Painters deal in realism – no one else does, Fulvio. Abstraction, Fulvio: it's air. You don't find out truth, reality, by watching guys – in and out of doors they go... It's meaningless.'

'You're right, Mack,' Fulvio says. 'In a way. But you are in the scene of cash, sex, favours – concrete stuff. Not reality – you don't need believe in that.'

'Invention,' Mack says, 'That's my scene?'

'You have to play antique to figure in it,' Fulvio says. 'You need to have had a mother, know how to cry and curl your lip, and break up with your girl, your boy. The rest, though, is all yours.'

'I surf on information,' Mack says...

'But don't fall in,' Fulvio finishes. 'Expressionism – that is part of all of us. Even the Nibelungs knew that, though you should avoid their fate. Then there's surrealism – remember, there's true and false out there, for sure it's of no account, you can't tell them differently, and remember – act on neither. But think "surreality": how'd you distinguish truth in there?'

'Expression too,' says Mack, gathering speed. 'How d'you tell the true in that? Can you have false abstraction?'

'Why not?' asks Fulvio. 'You'd have to wait and see, and that you need not do. In fact – *davai, davai* – on, on! Don't look back! Forget your gender, colour, class – they only matter if they're monetised, or if you slap them on the scale like cod.'

'Yes,' says Mack. 'Action! I remember those Italians, the cult of the bald brow, the jutting chin... true and false – it all depends if you act on something. Then, there's consequences – but they don't prove a thing. Experience is out! There is no test, no authenticity – it's all in numbers, all there is is them, lined up, you, left to spin a tale... You were right – it's *facho,* but who cares – if everyone is doing it... Action, Fulvio, try it out, see if it fills a need.'

'Yes, Mack,' says Fulvio, 'but don't convince me. I'm gullible, I believe all that you say, until I find some process that will change my mind.'

'Changing minds – that's my destination; since we don't know what minds are, it should be simple, Fulvio,' and Mack's convinced.

'Don't believe me, Mack, but trust me. Right is with me, cleave to me, it will be yours too,' says Fulvio.

'I'm sure I can,' says Mack. 'I'm sure there's people just like me, who don't know where they'll end and how, but need to feel the right is always with them.'

'One day,' says Fulvio. 'You'll climb that stair, and force the iron door, go up the flight that opens out before you, and leave the smell behind...'

'Why not,' says Mack.

'Feel how springy the ground here is,' says Fulvio, flexing his knees and bouncing, although he's standing on the carpet... 'It's that kind of moss, sphag something... You must be sensitive to things – we can do so much damage, in our job, so many people we don't know about, and care still less...'

'It's marshy,' Mack says. 'That liquid makes the green unnatural, like boiled stuff – artichokes, perhaps. I know – we must be strong, and speak our minds. We're experts, we must do the best for everyone...'

'We must be strong and choose,' says Fulvio. 'There's no best decision, no best advice – there's precision, and there's drift, that's all. For every stranger that gets hurt, be sure, there's one of ours...'

'Oh,' says Mack, 'you can't think ours and theirs. Or quantities. It's what is right, least harm...'

'Really Mack!' says Fulvio. 'This isn't right. If what is best is greatest harm – it often is – that's what must be done. That is consistent, and consistency – that is important, a priority. Not taken for granted, obviously – but what's to be done – is often the most radical, the obvious, the root...but not the branch. Roots – rooted out. The branch – is quite irrelevant. The root's what counts.'

'At first,' says Mack, tilting on his heels. 'I hadn't seen how deep it went – when Sophie recommended me, I'm sure she didn't see how it would be a test, reaching to the centre of our brains...'

'Be strong,' says Fulvio, 'and then you can do the rest.'

★

That committee – starts as a trick, goes on as puzzle. Mirror – and doorway too. Mack gathers friends, as though he's smeared with syrup, or with tar. It's good to be so rich – some countries you can help with pills, or taking in your dirt ... others you condone, others still you arm, you bomb... It's not by chance, nor malice ... everybody knows everything, that committee – it's open as the sky, anyone can be a cloud, a bird – eagle or dove...

'It works like this, the world,' says Fulvio. 'Now you know, don't let it hold you up. You've finished here – this way, you've seen, we gain immortality. We're part of the design. You win, you lose, you take a nap. It spins along. The aim is – not to drop from rich – a varied income – to poor. The rest is shaking hands or having them blown off.'

'Something is missing here,' Mack says. 'I understand the stagecoach and the pony express – that's history. Where's the abyss?'

'Oh,' says Fulvio. 'You can ride slow to that. Not many Indians left. Concentrate on being lifelike. Develop.'

'Develop?' asks Mack. 'Sex and psychology? Must I have those?'

★

Sylvia says, 'They're trying to dump me too. We're important now – we are the globe. We get to say what's real – above us there is only strategy.'

The afghans have gone.

'We could change everything, then?' says Mack.

'Are you really interested?' Sylvia asks. 'You seem to think of other things. I wonder what comes after dogs ... my space is limited. See how they chewed my shoes!'

Her bare feet are tempting, youthful.

'Don't be misled,' says Sylvia, as Mack looks at her map: good guys, bad, indifferent, with little blue patches scattered: 'dogs'. 'It's much more complicated, Mack, you see,' she says. 'Haven't you grasped anything? We're down as "indifferent" – didn't you do cosmology at school?'

'I thought Fulvio was my friend,' says Mack. 'I've just about resigned...'

'Oh,' Sylvia says. 'Fulvio wants to be top dog. Mine were the same.'

She pats a space for Mack beside her on the couch. They sit in silence.

'Maybe you'd like to see me in my jewels?' says Sylvia: 'your eyes, Mack, rest them for a while.'

She doesn't have a lot of jewels. Without her clothes, you see them, though – they shine, a necklace and a ring.

What happens – it's a surprise, but it's familiar too. 'You see,' says Sylvia, 'The best of worlds.'

'I must have missed that day at school,' says Mack.

'We could have had some music too,' says Sylvia, pouring jasmine tea.

'That's a beautiful necklace,' Mack says. 'I'm not usually into jewellery, but ... I could get away with wearing it...'

'Let that be our secret,' Sylvia says. 'Though a secret between two – it's in a limbo.'

'We've saved a lot of people, Sylvia,' Mack says. 'We might say our responsibility's discharged.'

'Discharged? Or just at half cock?' Sylvia asks. 'Here, take the necklace...'

'I shan't fight on,' says Mack. 'Two of us can't win our places – two experts is a nonsense. We always disagree, dear Sylvia – you save the guys that I condemn, and so, and so. One of us – is always wrong. I leave the track to you... It's not my place to judge...'

'That's noble, Mack,' she says. 'You enjoyed my skin – it's right that you should leave my bones to clack in that long room, those shelves, the lines of shiny skulls we must pretend we cannot see...'

'They're our illumination, Sylvia,' says Mack. 'Mementoes. Spent bulbs. The thoughts they had are swirling round... You're a metaphysical – you must know.'

Like dust. Maybe – bacteria. Both have that thought, but neither brings it out.

*

'With you wandering on your adventures,' Fulvio tells Mack. 'You can't interfere. We can give our side schools, bombs too. Those others – quite the wrong kind of prelates, or suchlike... Guys who don't smile, or who smile too much. The demagogues, philosophers! They're tricky – you can fail as a putschist or revolutionary – philosophers can't fail: nor can demagogues.'

'Religion?' Mack asks. 'I didn't know you had one, Fulvio. But now it seems to be your world.'

'Oh, it isn't that,' says Fulvio. 'And nothing says it's progressive now. It's their friends.'

'I thought you were my friend,' says Mack. 'And now there's Sylvia, somewhere in-between...'

'The best friends,' Fulvio says, 'are those you hardly know.'

'When all our cash is spent, will they help us?' asks Mack.

'That's not the sort of question you should ask,' says Fulvio. 'Go somewhere carrying no cash, and see if someone helps you.'

'Oh, someone does,' says Mack: 'Always. But not enough.'

THE TOP DOG: WOLF

'You must call me Wolf,' says Wolf. 'Our local names are long and scurrilous. I'm a metaphysical – probably your friends are too... All's grist! I see you've plucked a leaf. On your head, it's a weak shield, but serves: Crusoe killed goats for hats. Savagery! It's true, the sun's a sulphurous flame – the leaf is ersatz, but just let me pry... Sometimes there's a rare spider hidden, conned like you...'

'And if there is?' asks Mack.

'Oh, we put it in a jar,' says Wolf, patting the rubbery leaf back on Mack's head.

'Our nature needs a hand,' says Wolf. 'We're chastened, naturally: it's new, protected, chaste, for ever, for as long as that may be... We made it all – the beasts, the trees, the flying things – a surface finely wrought, with artifice and calculations – a surface chased, as though it were a sheet of ice we've skated on...'

'It's all false?' Mack asks. 'All science? The birds taped, automatic, like they used to be at court? The beasts...'

'Of course, if they all eat one another, it's counter-productive,' Wolf laughs. 'They have the food that suits. We share our water with the trees...'

'It all sounds, well – banal,' says Mack. 'As if it comes out of a book.'

'Of course,' says Wolf. 'Don't be so philistine. We must defer to a necessity, and as we bow – we bite its knees. We must outrun the fates, Mack... All's fair.'

'My scene has none of this concoction, Wolf,' says Mack. 'I live as if I came from slime, or maybe egg. My body's all my own, I battle happenstance, I snap the causal chain when it seems opportune...'

'You have it wrong, Mack,' Wolf says, pissing on a treeroot. 'You think we've lost. Instead – we've won. The battle's fought, Mack, not by such as you, struggling in the tempest – but making a world we've devised ourselves. Control, Mack! That's what we have.'

'It seems arid,' Mack says. 'Hot.' Sweating.

'You have it wrong,' Wolf repeats. 'The point of being here is not to suffer chance and call it liberty. It's domination of everything that isn't us, made, chased, arabesqued and damascened... limned by us...'

'But will it last?' asks Mack.

'Beside the point,' says Wolf. 'At any moment stars explode, a rock extinguishes, continents submerge, a virus on a ramp kills all that moves... The point is – winning: not eternity.'

'Let's chat in your hut, Wolf,' says Mack.

Wolf's house has live birds on the roof, and beautiful ones in golden cages, an otter in the blue pool.

'I feel like Candide,' says Mack. 'Though I don't remember what its point was.'

'If you have arty friends,' says Wolf. 'Bring them over. They're welcome...'

'There's Aurora,' says Mack, wondering whether... 'She's into the *concrète*...'

'Oh, that's more grist,' says Wolf. 'Visiting artists. Exchanges. The world is one, Mack. The local poetry is very simple, but you'd not understand a word. We'd appreciate a challenger, though I doubt she'd sell.'

'It's not books, Wolf,' says Mack. 'Nor discs – it comes, as they say "from the elbow".'

'All the things they say!' says Wolf. 'Don't believe it. Especially as you're outside the culture...'

Kids stand to attention as Wolf and Mack stride into the classroom. 'They're doing state capitals,' says Wolf. 'Now Mack. Wichita. Tell us.'

Mack doesn't know. 'I'm very ambitious, Wolf,' he says. 'Convince me of something – I'll rise to the top, and get it done.'

'Be careful, Mack,' says Wolf, laughing. 'That's true of scum: that rises – it's dregs that don't.'

'Ambition makes up for not knowing much,' says Mack.

'Know people,' Wolf says solemnly. 'Drink with them. Drink them under. Now – shall we go down the mine? Or see what I have put on ice?'

That cold tomb's full of tequila – special, raw.

Then down the hole they go – a yellow bore: the cage – a lobster pot. 'Don't dangle out your arms and legs,' shouts Wolf – all the way down, there's roots of things that's given up, no resurrection and no flower, no fruit... It's sea-cold now. Skins, shells – pelicans who dived too far, turtles capsizing... 'Suppose it all falls in!' shouts Mack.

The cage twists round and round – and are those bones? 'Up, up!' shouts Mack. 'What if the rope...?'

'Sometimes there is that effect,' says Wolf. 'A flashback – probably the drink. You didn't see the galleries, the lights, the guys white-suited and whistling – in the cage, projections of *La Bonne Année*. It's Lelouch, I'm almost sure...'

'I didn't see all that,' says Mack, 'You're right. I saw things long ago. State capitals ... can't think how I didn't know...'

'Oh, young Hossein gets them all right,' says Wolf: 'He's our best student. Very cosmopolitan.'

'What could I do for you, good Wolf?' asks Mack.

'Nothing,' says Wolf. 'I'm not a predator. I'm Wolfgang – but I have no gang! I'm the only wolf round here,' and he laughs. 'One thing – limes. That would be of use.'

'Limes?' asks Mack. 'You mean *limes* – frontiers?'

'My Latin's better than yours, dear Mack,' says Wolf. 'I mean limes.'

'And your friendship is secure,' says Mack. 'Anything modest you might want...'

'Just things as they are,' says Wolf. 'No change, no meddling required. Oh – and a bird organ – to teach birds how to sing... Look in your store. It has a handle. Better than the real thing, Mack, easy to pack...'

'I'm on my way upwards, Wolf,' says Mack. 'I'll see you get your fruit. Another message...?'

'Tell Fulvio, and your – my – other friends, a sad sad fact. The people – how we believed in them! – has failed. Politically. Tell them, Mack, have them reflect.'

It's true, Mack thinks: Wolf – is like the other bigs. He's been what he is for years – and now the rest are copying him. Ur-type – Alexander, Timur, Bonaparte... On a smaller scale, for sure. He's better than them, too – he's an aesthete. They'll ask me about the stereotypes – but you can't importune your host – "show me some poor people, the desperate ones – maybe those defrauded by some boss..." They're there, I'm sure.

*

'Remarkable cities, Fulvio,' says Mack. 'Next time, give me an assistant – I'll bring you back more tales. All's marble – the statues are of gold. They've Painters too – they don't paint, they sell, and they know everything. The orgies...'

'Orgies are old hat,' says Fulvio. 'And vulgar too. Not every boss is keen on them. Me – I have my friends dress up and re-enact the histories. In wigs, with claymores, gossip, poisoners – we have an evening's fun, a bit ridiculous, but staid – and then to bed – each as they choose, with or without. History, dear Mack, is mostly sex, and then revenge. It's like the dice – you roll with what you've got, those dots are fixed, they're pokerwork: – your territory's allotted now. It's a bore to change the boundaries – the *limes* as they're called: you're better digging down and drilling – deeper, deeper, till from warm you go to hot. The magma, Mack! That's where we're destined...'

'Oh yes,' says Mack. 'We spoke a lot of that – the heat, the missing fruits. The limits. Of course, they have their ancestors, manic dancing, snorting stuff up straws – it's alien, but exactly what you've read about... And Wolf's a gentleman. Why, I could take Aurora...'

'We'll put him on the good guys list,' says Fulvio. 'Forget Aurora. She's our treasure, she stays here.'

'It's worth knowing Wolf,' says Mack. 'The more he digs – down to the core – the more he's central, Fulvio. A sensitive place like that, already prepared for what comes after the abundance – it could led to envy: war. Or – it could save us all.'

'What might it be?' asks Fulvio, and laughs.

'There's unexpected things,' says Mack. 'It needs a twist, a scrip they used to say – a substance, gives a hope, or just makes a scene, a product never dreamed of... People could start going there, making the locals rich ... or else the stuff's strategic, and there's terror there for all...'

'Well, that doesn't tell us much,' says Fulvio. 'But – perhaps, if something has a centre, it is there: Wolf's land. But forget about Aurora. She's a poetess, a medium – she's gone beyond words, only aficionados bother with her. She's a party piece. Don't be taken in...'

'Oh, I'm not,' says Mack. 'Anything in words – it's been said, over and over. So – beyond words – their sounds – it's meaningless, or obsolete. When I was small...'

'You had the rage, and screamed with nonsense words...' Fulvio finishes – 'So what? Who didn't? That's syndrome, it's not character.'

'Aurora sings,' says Mack. 'The poems without words – maybe "deep words" – she sets to music. It is quite a fad – it makes many different kinds of sense...'

'She's not an assistant for you, Mack,' says Fulvio. 'She is for here, not there.'

'It's personal,' says Mack.

'Oh, you're beyond all that,' says Fulvio. 'You are in charge now. You don't have a personal. Besides, Wolf's people sold the animals as trophies, used the cash to pay for artificial ones. Those golden statues – a superspecies, no doubt with humps, a goitre...'

'Oh Fulvio,' says Mack. 'There's so much rubbish talked about the animals. Each is for each – maybe an egg for continuity: the idea of species they don't have. Nature's classification, that is all. Your schema, yours alone. Tough that we ate them in huge quantities, better we can do without, eat chops that taste like theirs.'

'Those golden statues,' Fulvio says. 'They're worrying. The lumps – maybe they're muscle packs. Or could they be a memento, memento mori?'

'That's what they are,' says Mack. 'They come from movies. Muscles and early death. The people go wild for them – they're still into heroes – heroines don't count at all.'

*

'Paco's room – without him, it's clean and bare. It looks quite decent: with less – there's more, more care, more of tomorrow,' Mack says. 'I'm waiting for Aurora. She could do her show – somewhere they'd appreciate a piece of art with class.'

Maybe this stranger, this new woman, doesn't understand – she could be casual, it doesn't look like here's a squat, her being partner of a team – she could be Algerian, Anouk. The kohl's a giveaway. Mack spies – behind the shades, her eyes – elaborate. She has a kefiyah, dark glasses, the scarf up to the glasses' edge. Maybe from Tlemcen – or no! Don't speculate – too poor for those plump weddings, white horses, reds and yellows, maybe anyway not one of them, those families... She opens up her face – the glasses off, kefiyah furled.

'Aurora's a wonder,' says Anouk. 'She's so inventive.'

Mack stands by the window, with Anouk. So close – they can smell each other, so close: both a-quiver. Aurora didn't get in through the glass, that last time: today it's raining. He puts his arm through Anouk's – it's risky, as if he's escorting her somewhere... A gesture natural, but obsolete. 'Escorting,' he says. 'Now, that means a kind of prostitute – the days when it meant something else, courteous, deferring – those have gone. I guess it was paternalistic too. Sexist – like a handcuff built into a suit.'

'Oh,' says Anouk. 'Days – those have all gone. It's coming, time, but not yet cut up into lengths, not anything, no people with a gender and their clothes all set and matching.'

'I hope Aurora shows up soon,' says Mack. Really, he doesn't. It's a risk, Anouk leaves him – and Aurora may turn up: she leaves him tongue-tied. She's creative, and she shows it off. She wants everything – nothing, really from Mack or anyone – it could never be enough, nor too little...

'People, Mack,' says Anouk. 'You're like everybody – you think people save you, put flesh on your bones. It isn't so – they pull you down.'

'Ours is already a relationship,' says Mack. 'What can that signify?'

'Oh, sex,' says Anouk. 'That's where the curiosity lies. Now that peep-shows are closing down. Should I tell you about my family?'

'No,' says Mack, 'That's gossip. Literature. Peace and war. I'm interested in the real thing – a country. A state, betting on the next card.'

'Are you sure?' Anouk asks. 'It could be a con.'

'That's the challenge, Anouk,' says Mack. 'Aurora – with her sounds, those roars without language, just words – it's my idea to see if something universal works...'

'Of course it does,' says Anouk. 'It's sense is limited, that's all. It's somewhere between music and the word of God. Of course she'll be understood. But – is it worth it?'

'I have difficulties,' says Mack. 'This isn't really what I want to do... Some people find me irresistible...' and he thinks of Sylvia, and of Fulvio – 'others, probably.'

'I don't think it's that,' says Anouk. 'It's your gullible expression. You're easy to slough off. Your mind's elsewhere – that doesn't help you hold a course.'

'For that,' says Mack. 'You need be in the cold, on the waves. Stars and winds.'

'You talk like you don't belong in a particular space,' Anouk says, cradling his face and examining it like it was a plate of food. 'You should be an architect. Rebuild a capital.'

'Yes,' says Mack, enthused. 'Away with all that public void, the promiscuity, the squares where strangers gather, wheel and flee like starling clouds, the newspapers blowing dusty up and down, like in that grounded spaceship... Back to the warmth: twisted alleys. Lairs for cutpurses. Budgies on fake trees pulling tarot cards... peep-shows, roasteries, parrakeets, guys filling cartridges and straightening trombones. Black gutters flowing to the fields. Houses built on mud, houses emaciated, houses windowless. Cops in half uniforms, laundry dripping on your head... You're right, Anouk. That's what I'd build. No statues – maybe a plaque – my name spelled wrong, no date of death. Guys on cane chairs playing the *tar*.'

'I could live there, Mack,' says Anouk, 'Maybe I did.'

'The space is terrifying,' Mack goes on. 'Those squares – a maquette of the electric space around us all, those dead voices – do they sing, or do they squeak?'

'You could ask,' says Anouk. 'Aurora – that sounds like her world... The nightingale – taking no room.'

'You're right, Anouk,' says Mack. 'Maybe there's a sarcastic edge. Art stands at its angle to it all...'

'Tripping like that, Mack,' says Anouk. 'It's art that tumbles... Space moves on, dwindles, swells – here come the soldiers and the tanks...'

'Now, Anouk, that goes too far,' says Mack, laughing. 'They were always there, marshalled in the *place d'armes*. You need have one of those, or it isn't real. Now – there's a space that really isn't: – always full of wheeling and commands.'

They walk together – 'They hate it, being poor,' says Mack. 'My construction. But they all muck in – some of them. They hate it, though, the being poor.'

'Yes,' Anouk says. 'I smell it, their hate. It's good, it's paprika. They'll do something with the hatred, even though their lives are fucked.'

'They'll need to face the neighbours,' Mack says. 'The violent ones. Houses with fresh stucco. The ones who beat them, drug them, sell them to the cops. There is nothing to be done.'

'Well, anyway, Mack,' Anouk says. 'You'll have built the right place for it all.' She laughs, and so does Mack. 'It's design too,' she says. 'Trees for the parrots – and their toys. I bet you'll do the music, and the dance.'

'Of course,' says Mack, 'you don't just see the houses – there's the smell, kids running – everything at once. You have to put it in.'

'Aurora?' Anouk asks. 'It's her I came to see. So, do you put her in? It's a century since concrete poetry began – and birds were always doing it, and better still... If she's a metaphor, she's wingless, nesting on the earth. A lark, no more.'

'It's discovering an island,' Mack says. 'Cuba, always there, but always meaning different things. It's not the sounds Aurora makes – it's her conviction. The clothes, the nakedness beneath that she's so proud of, that she'll miss when it no longer can attract...'

Anouk says, 'As I was coming here – a soldier stopped me. I was covered up. I didn't want to show: not that I wanted to do bad things to people that I didn't know. Maybe it's easier to hurt a stranger than a friend – it's all beyond me...'

'Oh,' says Mack, 'We do it all the time. Something good or bad to everyone. My group: our hurting is offset by all the good we do – especially to our friends. But – Anouk: this talk is infantile. Of course you know how we've set up the world.'

'It's not you, Mack, this judgment talk,' Anouk says. 'You're not a person if you rise above the rest. What keeps you there – sex and flattery?'

'Life is sticky, Anouk,' says Mack, embarrassed. 'Rules and punishment came in early for us all. Religion or not – just being here, modern or shaman – the rules draw stage coaches full of punishment. That shamanistic poet – Ali something – was religious, and went down to hell, a frequent traveller: but goodness! The punishments! The rationales, his vendettas! There's no escape, Anouk. If you don't do it, someone will to you! If that is poetry – better don't fit words. That's Aurora's message.'

'Which you ignore,' says Anouk, quite fondly.

'Ah well,' says Mack. 'There's no words!'

*

'There's words!' Anouk says. 'We're stuck with them. She's a golem, Aurora – on her forehead "Truth": – erase a letter, and it's "Death". That is the wall, the glass wall, that bounds you, Mack. Death.'

'Of course,' says Mack. 'It is the boundary stone. For everything. Look! – there's one in the maquette. We can't be miniature, not like the drab reclusive nightingale, walk in those tiny streets – but if we can't go where you've designed, there's thousands of streets still, like what you've built, where we might go. It isn't difficult. It's like Paco – finishing off the worthy films. Down the alleyway we go, Black and white, all paid for, and then – there is the fight... A gang's upon us – the unreflecting clubs! our clockwork unwinds, we struggle, the organs wail and fail.'

'Paco is right,' says Anouk, 'about the ends. Might he perhaps tack on new beginnings to them all, make them his masterpieces?'

'It's a nice conceit, Anouk,' says Mack. 'But we're always late in, at the movies. We never see the start. True, Paco's not derivative – but those endings! All the same. All true. No, he doesn't have it in him, not to make different beginnings. We've always missed the prelude – we end the same, just like he says. But so – we always start the same as well, somewhere in between: the middle. Someone else has written in the middle part...'

'You're wrong,' Anouk says. 'Once we had work, the work was what we were. The droughts, the marsh gas, canaries coughing, oxen on their knees... Now – we think we can become what we are paid to do... It's true, it's false. We take crap jobs – "It's temporary – tomorrow I will learn the tricks that liberate my genius..." It isn't so, Mack. We are temporary, worth no more: from zero job to crap incontinence and poverty.

'The movie – should be short, if it's to be true: an opening shout, a final croak, and in between – white light. A waiting unfulfilled, purposeless. You become – suspension. Pure expectation... There is no story, Mack. So, Paco's right: take the eraser – truth... one letter less...'

'Oh,' Mack says, and laughs, 'but you are free, Anouk! No history! No disillusion, no politics, no thwarted lives. Just lives lived, start to end. Years and years of them.'

'Let's go in the maquette,' says Anouk. 'Or go where it's real because it's large, like us. A life-sized replica. We shouldn't need to bend, not go on all fours to enter. The fields are huge, untended, full of inedible grass. See – how the houses lean, support each other... If the last one isn't stone – down we all go!'

'Those houses, Anouk – they're strong...' says Mack: 'The sills are diorite, Makonde slate upon the floors ... all looted...'

'It's all the rest,' Anouk says. 'The walls, the doors. Those shut you out, they fall, they smother you.'

*

They're much too big – they can't get in the maquette. The real is slightly different. 'There's Wolf's residence far off,' says Mack. 'It's his Chambord. The prey runs all around, and he has towers with lozenges, blind arches, like in those nursery building sets. No salamanders, not like that French guy, the boss did jail time down in Spain – what's Wolf's badge, I wonder...'

'Maybe it's the jackal,' Anouk says. 'They're discreet. True, they don't live on fire, regenerate the air, and swim ...

salamanders are the best, for sure. The jackal's canny, it adapts. Life is fighting over carrion, for ever more. It seems Wolf's hunkered, prepared for other wars – not the big one yet, but loud bangs far away. You say – the only thing he lacks is limes? He can last out a siege with those...'

'It's *limes*,' Mack insists. 'Limits must be respected. He would build a wall around his park, and sit inside. But – he needs the rest of us, though he'd prefer to keep us out. Even if it's just for fruit. I'd be an idiot, to come back with a bowl of fruit, as if I hadn't twigged...'

'The houses here,' says Anouk. 'They're not like your imagination – they're low, they bulge with daub, the roads are wide, the soil – is yellow, pink – like lemons, pomegranates.'

'Of course,' says Mack. 'You can't imagine everything. It's variations. Fruit – is at the root.' They laugh, and there's no echo – it just goes up and up, the sound.

'Are you a variation, Mack – or do you want to be a theme?' asks Anouk asks. 'Or just another jackal?'

'I have people ranged behind me, Anouk, people who push me to the top...' says Mack.

'Is there a top?' Anouk asks. 'What do they, do you, get from the manoeuvring?'

'A spacious story,' Mack says. 'A chance you won't end strung to a tree, hung by your heels.'

'Well,' says Anouk, agreeing. 'Forget the stuff you were taught about counting costs, counting heads, and being kind. Did it work?'

'Oh,' says Mack. 'I'm modern enough. I discard what doesn't suit.'

'You can be kind to me,' Anouk says. 'But Wolf? Does he need a philosophy, and run the risk it sets?'

'He's discounted it,' says Mack. 'He wants for almost nothing. His park, his hunting – he has that safe. All he needs now, is to dig. There's always something underneath. You've got the cash up front, at any rate, if you don't strike...'

'Mack,' says Anouk. 'It's quiet. No one can spy. May I say, you have a fault. You tumble – and you think that shows your destiny is up, is upwards. It isn't so, my friend...'

'Betrayal, Anouk, that's the worst,' says Mack. 'The point is not where you may end, but who you've shafted on the way. I try to keep my purity...'

'You're right, Mack,' Anouk says. 'That is *my* fault. Done in a determined way – for my security, denouncing ... cops and cash ... the whole scenario. I am impure.'

'I'm sure you'll be forgiven,' Mack says, not bothered.

'Is that what I want?' Anouk asks. 'Or need. And who? Forgive? Excuse? Forget? Who sits on my case? Someone better, someone worse, someone objective? It happens all the time, the Genghiz syndrome – deciding destinies of people you know nothing of... Comes in all sizes – from a massacre to a sneak. Once done ... for all time, it's finished.'

'If something's irresolvable,' says Mack. 'It's not a problem.'

'So I'll go on, do it all again?' says Anouk.

'It's probable,' says Mack. 'Now – the people will come back from the grassy fields, the birds will start to sing again... A nothing world, music and cooking, until it's dark, then sleep. There's no beasts left. That grass – if the experiments go well, we'll all be eating it, digesting it, like it was lobster claws.'

'My spying, betraying,' Anouk says. 'It could be a something between us – do you think? And yet – anyone can do it, however willing, or unwilling...'

'Of course!' says Mack. 'It's not a gender question, nor faith, conviction – age, class – anything you can think of. Betrayal – is the universal. Even history does it – avalanches of people; ideas falling from the tomes like bookmarks, all forgotten, turning upside down like tumbling leaves. A something, a barrier – what would it mean between us? There's so many things that are or aren't impediments ... walls, windows, structures, transparencies, meniscus celluloid...'

'Yes.' Anouk says. 'But – we're made to be small islands – waterless, nothing edible, but bounded. The sterile sea – our guarantee, defence. We're all a fortress, full of holes. Without each one of us being confined within a wall, a barrier – a skin – the outside would be the death of us.'

'Well,' says Mack, and laughs. 'It often is. That's what you've found out! What they call "the abyss of terror" – it can be the island next to you! Or your dearest friend, of course.'

'This place,' says Anouk, 'isn't Africa – but it's full of Africans.'

'Let's sit down here,' says Mack, 'and wait till they've all come back from work. Capitalism – it can't produce, but lets you roam. You're not a resource, a richness – if you can't find cash, or borrow – best move around, leave what isn't ever home. Relax, Anouk. Maybe they'll serve us something for the heat – a juice, a vodka chilled – we'll only need decide... As for this place – let's not conclude what's good or bad, who's borrowed what, or invented from pure air and brain... If I manage to master this, this site – its outs and ins – I'll be an expert on a continental scale, Anouk.'

'You said Wolf is the master,' Anouk says. 'This work you do – it's your Ingres violin... There's many who assist the falling and the fallen... I'd call that work, Mack; yours is dilettantism...'

'You're wrong, Anouk,' says Mack. 'What we might do – is resolve a problem; not bring aid, bind up the wounds... Might what we do bring the result we want? We know it can't...'

'Ending problems would be one thing, Mack,' says Anouk. 'What you guys do is satisfy your interest, just short term.'

★

The guy who brings the vodka says he's an engineer. He sits beside them – 'That "grass", you call it, Mack,' he says. 'It could be wonderful. Maybe you like fiddleheads? ... well, that's the aim...'

'I guess it could be modified,' says Mack. 'You could put bromide in it. or that stuff – demerol? Is that it?'

'There's lots of work to do,' the guy says. 'But so far – no one digests it. It still takes a lot of care just to have it grow, mature.'

'The traders here,' Anouk says, 'don't come from here.'

'No,' the guy, Adolphe, says. 'But they've always been here – much longer than the ones who come from here.'

'Pepper,' Anouk says, quite loudly, repeating, louder still. 'Pepper! Fields of it, the little red hot horns, Pan the devil, in his hairy pants... When we all worked in the fields – there was peace, there was the true religion. Terrible! Disaster! Oh, how I understand the dream of freedom: being free is squalid, they chase you, beat you: being free, it bears no fruit, you leave no canvas, no whittled stick carved out with hooves and tail, no hut, no ring of stones, no wreath of marjoram... Free people? In their carts, limp targets, running. Freedom! You smoke it in your cutty pipe, the smoke ... that's what rose up: how I understand, the Man of Steel who sees them dancing round, the sluggards and the bullies, the lilywhites – smoke, soot and sludge, you live in chalcedony, they surround you, you must put them down, every last one, then – you'll be free... Even if it's only you. *Especially* just you, the one who understands. Except ... the road up there is flint and ice, Adolphe'

'There's no pepper vodka, Anouk,' Mack tells her. 'This is the best there is – it's not so good.'

'I want Wolf to be like that,' Anouk goes on, ignoring him. 'Destroying everyone around him – until there's only she that's left, chimera, trans, gryphon: free. And so you cut its head off – that's the way!'

'It's the underground,' says Adolphe, quite bemused. 'Everyone – having a go. A festival.'

'You're mistaken, Anouk,' Mack says, forcing her back in her chair. 'These guys – if they go against Master Wolf – it isn't to be free! They may resent oppression – but even if they've some success – they are not free. They work, perhaps. They don't produce – they float. Their ambition – stasis.'

'You realise,' says Adolphe, impatiently. 'That if the grass experiment succeeds – we all will come to bring forth milk. And not just milk – we'll have the life, the system, that lets us make kefir, and cheese – the red, the blue, the orange. That is our destiny, beyond philosophy. Beyond the disciplines: self-sufficiency.'

'Adolphe,' says Mack, 'many humans have always produced their milk and fed their kids – even if they'd eaten steaks.'

'Oh,' says Adolphe. 'Now – it would be everyone. All their lives, and other aspects too – more placid, life in herds...Milkmaids too, I guess.'

'I'm unconvinced,' Mack says. 'Clans, herds – it's quite banal, Adolphe, a commonplace: your insight doesn't fly. And people don't want to be free, Anouk – they want sufficiency. All your philosophy is metaphysical: that's been snuffed out. Wolf wants his privilege, is all: autonomy – in other words – sufficiency.'

'Oh, Master Wolf,' says Adolphe. 'He's not a monster, not concerned with soot and mud, accumulation – nothing like, robbing banks, making a state and running it – he is benevolent, and idle too. You've seen his ranch, the furniture he makes from kits ... the birds wired up, that make no mess.'

'It will come,' says Anouk. 'It's a raptus, a rabies, it's our rage. Painting with blood – it's still painting. The arterial rush. Killing is abstraction, torture is a measured depiction – and it's never enough, never finished. When you've done your masterpiece – it's just one of Bluebeard's wives – there's thousands of them – up the driveway they come, some in the driving seat, some bound, chained in the trunk.'

'Well,' says Adolphe, fascinated by Anouk, 'Wolf's not like that at all.'

'No, I know,' says Anouk. 'No one can ever be Bluebeard, however hard they try, long to be up there, free. It's because it starts off sex – you'd never manage all those brides. At first, it's hidden. A harem behind the screen. Then – it's out! It's in the books! On the walls, in the salon... A challenge, a piece of tapestry. I know! I've been in all that. There is no blue beard in the end – it's hair and pigment. Everybody starts with hair – dye it with woad – and there you are!'

'Well, Anouk,' says Adolphe, unsure. 'Are you for it? What you say. Or maybe not?'

'Here I am, Adolphe,' Anouk says, calling for more white spirit: 'Find out what you can from me – I never conceal what I may know.'

'This pepper thing you have, Anouk,' says Adolphe, fascinated still.

'The red, the chili, pepper?' Anouk asks. 'You take one, put it in your *cul,* like so. It drives all day. To sleep, you take it out.' And she shows how.

'I'd heard the cops make use of them,' says Adolphe. 'I should tell Master Wolf. It would spur production on... The guys here sometimes run into the streets – "more cash" they shout. But what is there to buy?' he asks.

'That's not the point,' says Anouk. 'They might want to start a stall, and sell. The point is, Adolphe – all the stuff you see on coins, the useless ones they pass to you, "freedom, equality" – these have lost their sense. It's a part of the old religions, the "trust" for bosses: those used to fudge philosophy as best they could – now, there's no need. It's over, Adolphe. All that remains, is Mack: self justification. Rhetoric.'

'You've changed my life, Anouk,' says Adolphe. 'Maybe while you're here – you'd do a painting for our show? A song?'

'I could, of course,' Anouk says. 'But our friend, Aurora, that's her thing. She does it every dusk – spun into air, without reward, without regard, following the skein ... that leads to fate ... Euridyce, dear Adolphe. No – I might stay for the revenge that tips up Master Wolf, his heels a-waltzing in the air. Or else – his vengeance. None of that my pleasure, nor my fault. The best place to enjoy the sight...?'

'You're a monster, Anouk,' Adolphe says, with some admiration. 'I thought Mack was ambitious, but I see I was quite wrong...'

'Oh, Adolphe,' Anouk says. 'I want nothing. Mack can plot and screw – his vanity's unlimited. I want a finer thing. Height, Adolphe. The view – if possible, the panorama.'

'Remember,' Mack says. 'What I know. Every night, death lies beside you in the bed, whoever else you stock it with. And in the morning, there's the song: Aurora.'

'It sounds like casuistry,' says Adolphe, swept away by Anouk. 'There's no connection. And death lies still in your bed all day, and waits.'

'He needs a pepper up his arse!' says Mack, and they all laugh.

*

They're coming back from work, the fields. The people. Revolutions don't last long. 'The French chopped off its head,' says Mack. 'To be generous, maybe it fell before Moscow. Then the Muscovites – so long after – lost theirs against the Poles.'

'Every time they come back to their houses,' Adolphe says. 'There is a skirmish.'

Some look on, others throw rocks, run up and down. Some are dragged away.

'There'll always be the people,' Adolphe says, pulling down Anouk, who's climbed on her chair to watch. 'Until there aren't – and then there'll be no bosses either.'

Rocks and bouncing bullets come closer. 'There's nothing to be done,' says Adolphe, as they hide behind a tree. 'They want their land. An illusion! No one has land now. Besides, it's a drag: – the drought, the bugs, the prices and the lions... who'd want it?'

'I don't think there's lions,' says Mack.

'Maybe not,' Adolphe says, 'but I'm right about the rest.'

'They're determined,' says Mack. 'Remember when they said, 'Kill them all. God will recognise his own?' Are we come to that?'

'I never heard that,' Adolphe says. 'It doesn't seem germane.'

'There go the cops!' says Mack. 'It seems they've won again. Wolf's safe; besides, he isn't here.'

'Oh,' says Adolphe. 'He regrets all this – it's because he's what he is, not what he does. Or wants.'

'Well, Anouk,' Mack says. 'You're not concerned. Whoever wins – you're out of it. It was invention like we all do, your dealing with them, the betrayal, all that stuff, we've seen it many times, on the TV, in books: it's lost its sting.'

'Of course,' Anouk says. 'I am concerned. We all are, always.'

'You just came to see Aurora, found me,' Mack says. 'And so the story found its path.'

'I don't see any difference,' Adolphe puts in. 'Between us here, seeking shelter, and what Anouk says she once saw. Or did. It doesn't matter.'

'I never said a lie, Mack,' Anouk says, ignoring Adolphe. 'But if I did, so what? I'm not your memory. If things don't fit, you're not demented – and anyway, it all does fit.'

'You need something to hang on to,' Mack says. 'Otherwise you'd have nothing to let go of.'

'You let go, Mack,' Anouk says. 'Sure you'll float upwards. It isn't so. Down you go. It's easy, just the easiest thing.'

*

'Let's go back a bit,' says Adolphe. 'I'm interested in the drip technique, Anouk: you made the point about it being death: blood, a rain of blood. Chronology would fit, of course – after the Japanese campaign, the Bomb, Ardennes, all that. But can you take it further, the insight? – I hope it's not just limited to one technique...'

'Those guys here,' says Anouk. 'With the rocks, they should give up, move out. A few machines, some trusty hands – and all the rest won't have a job. Leave these crap dwellings, off ... bundles packed, feet forward...'

'It often goes that way...'Adolphe agrees –

'And who knows the fuck about this painting stuff?' Anouk asks.

'You haven't understood,' says Adolphe. 'It isn't about painting...'

'Of course I understood,' says Anouk. 'I said it! I can't answer your question, that is all.'

The road is full of rocks and burning tires. 'We can't get out,' says Mack. 'I should report all this. There's Fulvio and Sylvia – they'll need to recognise who's theirs...'

'There goes the nightingale,' says Anouk. 'Stupid bird. It sings, whatever. Indifferent, mechanical.'

*

'Master Wolf lets me sleep in his compound,' says Adolphe. 'You can't, of course. There is little sound – a fruit drops, a

pod bursts. There's harmony – you can add the emotions
on. The sonority goes through your bones and tweaks the
jelly in them. You'd not approve. Sleep in a hut, you two:
you'll hear the suck of tiredness, people sleeping, caught
between desire and quiet – they sleep like coils of rustling
wire ... the trucks would pass, hitting declivities and all
leaps up – the generators and the cutters, bulldozers and
their blades... There are no words aloud – those you see are
on the flourbags pinned out like otter skins, the flattened
cans of oil: sunflowers, Mack, the heat crushed out of them
to frizzling fry your dough.'

'I know,' says Mack. 'We shan't rest well. Those tin
walls – the rain a-galloping on the roof...'

'No rain,' says Adolphe. 'There's no need. There's
irrigation. Rain's a waste.'

*

'It's so cold,' Anouk says. 'Everything's been pressed,
milled, hammered, the heat – is liquid, then it's into you. A
pepper would be better, though.'

'Pull those flour bags over you,' says Mack. 'Nothing to
do with me, the cold, the hot. You're too honest, Anouk,
something like that: it all shows on your surface, the flow
throws it up – I can't get suckered in...'

'Adolphe is smart,' says Anouk. 'That's a shame. He
hasn't got a clue. In that compound – he could be dead,
and only Mastrer Wolf would know.'

'That's more than anyone would know of us,' says Mack.
'We two have no standing here.'

'No lying!' Anouk says. 'It's odd – to sleep you need to
lie. It's too cold for that here. You're white as porridge,

Mack, but maybe warm as well,' and she pulls him over her.

'This house, this hovel,' Mack says. 'You're part of it, sucked the heat from everything, and now from me.'

'Lying here,' says Anouk, 'I don't lie, you know – so that's a paradox! When you sleep, I wake, when you can't sleep – I do.'

'That's sentimental, Anouk,' Mack says. 'That's not like either of us.'

'No, it's not,' Anouk says, 'so, what's that big guy at the door? Is he epithalamium,' and she laughs.

The big guy says they can't find Adolphe: 'Nothing to do with me,' Mack says. 'There's riots here – the cops aren't interested in people, not singly: from outside – they just come and go.'

'You were together,' says the guy. 'And now there's two of you, not three.'

'I won't go to Master Wolf,' says Mack. 'Maybe there's destiny. To end like him? Or have him finish me...'

'Don't think about Master Wolf,' says the guy, pulling Mack by the arm. 'He's mute – it's the religion. Think about Adolphe. Clear it up.'

'Nothing's ever clear,' says Mack, resisting.

'Listen,' Anouk says. 'We talked about the drip of blood – maybe it gave him an idea? Or one he had already: a fear, its paws on his face as he's lying in the compound... And – who likes Master Wolf? Not many here...'

'I want to keep all that a mystery,' says Mack. 'My group... I can't be compromised...'

'Oh Mack, think big,' says Anouk. 'Take a side, take some responsibility. People get killed and disappear – it happens everywhere, there's provocation and there's opposition too – don't pretend you've no interest, no view...'

'Well,' says Mack, 'I guess I do – but Adolphe? He was bland... And who's this guy?'

'Adolphe was dull as family,' Anouk says. 'He could be rebel leader, Wolf's henchman – or just nobody at all in public – spitting on all of us as usual, lonely on his couch.'

'It's chance, Anouk,' says Mack. 'Meeting people, hearing of their deaths – at the level where we live – it's chance!'

'Well, Mack,' Anouk says, digging in her argument. 'You can't decide what's chance and what is your career – what's the alternative to chance, I ask? Order? Order is meaningless and arbitrary, there to be swept away – the places we're tossed through, never sticking for an hour – they twinkle like the bright stars and the dark, through the light and dark we flit, suffer a carom, compression, blooming, trailing sparks – we whirl away, no order, no control... If there is order, Mack, it's quite outside us – one and one, maybe it makes two everywhere, but like Engels said, two rabbits, given the right genitals, can make a hundred, maybe more...'

'Exactly, Anouk,' Mack says, as the tall guy, t-shirt made of flourbags roughly stitched, drags him from their hut – 'If it's not order, what's the alternative to chance? If all is chance and random – or set up according to some plan we must obey but never comprehend – what then?'

'If I understand,' the tall guy, Roman, says, 'no action can be meaningful if all is chance. So – if we say you made poor Adolphe disappear – we can ascribe no motive, you have no defence. Your actions, our deductions...'

'No, no,' shouts Anouk, 'this is juvenile. If matter moves, there's cause and there's effect. Mack was my blanket and at times my mattress too – all night my dreams are etched upon his skin...'

Roman pulls Mack's clothes off, just to ascertain: 'There's blood!' he shouts. 'Beneath!'

'It's mine!' shouts Mack.

'That is no proof,' says Roman, reasoning. 'It's dreams, you say, not blood, that shows your guilt or innocence.'

'Look,' Anouk says. 'It is a mystery: that's what people love. They like the puzzlement, the guessing at what's in the mind and all the tricksy steers to cheat the law ... Let Mack go free, and leave the mystery behind...'

It's a good deal. Maybe Anouk has used the argument before. Roman goes soft. Anouk's still stood before him, full of sleep and naked too – she's irresistible. 'A real man,' she shouts, 'would glimpse a paradise and let us go!'

Roman resists. 'Too many things we can't explain,' he says. 'You're right, Anouk. This is another one... You've made it all too deep for me.'

'You must always leave a clue,' Anouk says. 'Even if you hope no one will see until the end – remember, who can resist the charm of love? And isn't that the mystery, invoked when all else flops?'

'Anouk!' shouts Mack, 'You left the cold, went to the compound, sought out Adolphe – a flirtation I had never glimpsed...?'

'It often is that way,' Anouk says. 'In any case, where's Adolphe now?'

'Maybe you've trussed him, ready in your larder to consume,' Roman says. 'That's politics. From being cannibals, you evolve to praying things with myriad legs, their backsides full of silken ropes...'

'It's true, Roman,' says Mack, riddled with his jealousy. 'You think your future's clean, and then you see the parasites – got larger, gorged with your old expectations. Your belly – filled with aliens. Nothing to be done. That is the way...'

'The mystery,' says Roman, quite bemused, 'Seems to be solved. Everyone did what they did by chance. No one owns anyone or anything – the slogan's still "vote for the stupidest" – they'll have you fight their stupid wars, kneel in their temple, swing dancing on their rope.'

'Love is a poison,' Anouk says. 'The rejected lover – throws it in his lover's eyes. The last letter – burn it quick! Its smell will creep inside your shorts. You'll be arrested for necrophily. What was Adolphe? He cowered. Maybe he plotted victory, maybe he furled his flag and waited for the big parade... I lusted for his mind, his body – neat, white smooth, the kernel of a chicory. He wouldn't leave a mark – that was his gift. Given each day, freely and with fatuous tears, his soul, to Master Wolf.'

'That's where we stand, Anouk,' says Mack. 'I can't work out if you loved Adolphe, carried him off, or butchered him because he was so bland, hobbled, tied like a goat, clean, sterile...'

'Jealousy's a fine cloth,' Anouk says. 'It never wears. The colours – fast and faster, never run, they drag on, arm through your arm... It's muslin round your head, a turban and a veil...'

'The problem is,' says Mack, 'there's changes at the top. Security, Anouk. When we were strong, we punished bad guys, cosseted the good. Now, we've a guy on top. War, Anouk. There's two of them, he and his wife. Evil puppets, Roman and Anouk. They see our misery, distil it, pour it back on us. War, Anouk! That's what they talk about. Here, there, or everywhere... the nursery, Anouk, picking on some guy – imperative...'

'It isn't Paco's world,' Anouk says, terrified. 'But it's what he saw.'

'Sure, it was his world,' says Mack. 'Aurora's too. Dumb songs, wavering flicks – from fear. What use is warning? It will come, has come...'

'You must accept it, then,' says Roman. 'All that is, is valid, has its weight, and it will come to you, sit on your head and peck your eyes. What else did you expect?'

'Weak people want protection from the strong,' says Anouk. 'Even if the strong make them be oxen for the carts. There's no alternative – when the strong betray the weak there's been love, the charm of love, between them. Some will still believe in it. Wolf is strong – maybe he doesn't aspire to love. But – that's what he'll get, and then some will throw rocks...'

'It makes it difficult for me,' says Mack. 'Easy to win a fight against the weak... easy to dump a guy like Wolf... but if they have some kind of bond... Progressive grass, regressive rocks... and I've to give counsel to my boss...'

'Only you will find it difficult,' Anouk says, as they twist away from Roman, run off down the road.

*

'All sportsmen are buzz-heads,' says Fulvio. 'I don't understand it – you take a pill and fly, or a jug of grappa, do the hurdles – you win. That's that. Everyone takes dope or tunes their skeleton – so what? Trade souls with the devil for a silver cup... C'est la vie, Mack.'

'Oh, I agree, says Mack, 'but you can't bet on anyone and expect to win.'

'So – the bets I take,' says Fulvio, waving a gladstone full of cash, 'are on things we're all aware are full of dope... The political fix, the annual account, the ice core... Everybody knows it's fixed, so there's no squawk... It's the end of everything, and no doubt the start of something inconceivable.'

'But you're on the committee still?' asks Mack. 'I had a bad experience...'

'Even more so,' says Fulvio, 'I'm in the warm seat. The fix starts with the book, it always has. But – experience is neither good not bad, dear Mack. Grow up!'

'That's what they all say,' Mack says. 'I try to be judicious.'

'China,' Fulvio says. 'Billions of gamblers, no life insurance. They're our future. No bets on sports – but on the world: the air, the water. Relations of production, society, the system, bosses – all that stuff. You choose a period, and bet – yes or no. Going on or falling down.'

'Our zone, Fulvio,' Mack asks. 'Shouldn't we try to fix the odds on what we say ... our reasoning?'

'Oh, fiddle, Mack,' says Fulvio. 'That place is tiny where you went, and its fate ... it's the brown leaf, stuck on the tree... Will it fall off, fall this way, that? Be used for nesting or for lairs...? Who knows, Mack. The chances of this way, or that – it's mathematics, Mack. Pure chance. None can have interests in chance. No fix required.'

'You're crooked, Fulvio,' Mack says.

'Curved, Mack,' Fulvio says. 'Everything is: even nothing. Space is.'

*

'You seem to think you've a problem,' says Aurora. 'Please don't talk to me about it.'

'I have to be judicious,' Mack says. 'I quite like Wolf – he's like the guys you see, justifying, drawing in, a vision limitless, the pompous bastards... But really – I'm on the other side. I want to throw some rocks. I don't care who they hit, or what they do, the good, the bad – just throw them, hard.'

'All right,' Aurora says. 'That's good for you! Enough, though.'

She stands on one leg, and very very slowly pirouettes – the movement isn't smooth, you move your foot in tiny clocklike stabs. 'On stage,' she says, 'it looks like heaven, but doing it you think you've got it wrong. Mack – I won't say what you want to do is futile. That would seem I cast what *I* do in an arc of super brilliance. But – is that all? Do guys like you – do they really rule the world?'

Mack is silent, then. 'Where we were, me and Anouk: the big guy, Wolf – he had religion. Didn't want his boundaries, Aurora.'

'We're all getting it, or have it, Mack,' Aurora says, tilting forward till her nose touches the planks. 'Faith. The universal pretext. I bet you never saw it, the cult; never went inside, never fasted, burnt the stuff, inhaled, left your plastic sacrifice – maybe a telephone in case the angels called...'

'We didn't even eat,' says Mack. 'Not even milk and sandwiches, like the gods enjoy... Then there was Anouk – she's attracted to people, offers up herself... There was this guy who wanted justice, or at least a persecution: Roman... She displayed herself to him...'

'Everybody does that, Mack,' Aurora says. 'Everyone but you. You are relentless, you withhold yourself. We – all the rest – we want the other bodies near, the warmth, arms waved, our photos global, intercourse in front of millions...

Loosen up!' she says. 'Now, I have to up my act – why shouldn't you?'

'I put you in my future, dear Aurora,' Mack says, much saddened.

'My song is always at the last,' Aurora says, waving her arms. 'And in the dark. It comes after the future's done and been forgot.'

★

The group meets. Mack sits next to Sylvia – she touches his thigh, under the glass table. Then, she touches Fulvio's, the sight protected by his stack of files...

'If we befriend our Master Wolf,' the head guy, moderator, says, 'we make more enemies. If we befriend his enemies – we lose an ally. Unleash the massacres. If we do nothing, someone else will act. Now, Mack, what's your take? Just guide us through...'

'Eastern religions,' Mack starts off, 'they say they ruined Rome – I don't know how ... but the charm of love ... was like the thread that takes you out of hell, then breaks and drops you right back in, and now they're gripped by legends, beasts that talk and empathise, prospects of introspection without bounds...'

'The testimony that Mack brings,' says Sylvia, turning away. 'Is suspect. There's a report of robbery and murder, lovers exchanged, the fruits of friendship spurned or not delivered. Collusion, Mack!'

'Oh Sylvia,' Mack protests. 'Those fruits are always poisoned. Remember Captain Cook, the mutiny about the fruit, and Christian, the abandoned pilgrim...'

'Oh no!' shouts Sylvia. 'That Cook that boiled his crew?!' and she sobs...

'If you go sailing without charts,' says Fulvio wisely. 'You fall off the earth you love, and what you think you find resembles what you didn't want to know...'

'Fulvio is right,' the head guy, moderating, says. 'We might send backing clandestinely to both the sides... Maybe build a temple, stupa – wherever is the mystery...'

'Mack slipped with the poisoned apples,' Fulvio says, laughing. 'They took to opium instead.'

'That grass,' the head guy asks. 'Can it work in motors? Does it burn? Can we use it for our lights?'

'Of course,' says Fulvio, 'the guys that mow it – they put in their energy. Besides – there's more sun there, it powers things up: we might sell it as a drink. Our peoples – they're distracted, flabby, their time is running down... Be decisive, everybody! *On s'engage!*'

'There was sex, I hear,' says Sylvia. 'Mack, his assistant – everybody. Having it, or not. I guess it's natural. But – is it natural we live in houses, use dope, put on our mascara – is it natural that cassowaries live in cages, jackals too?'

'We can't lump everyone together,' the head guy says. '"Humans". What does that say? We're more refined – we need to know the pedigrees, affiliations...'

'People there,' says Mack, 'they had a substance, a gravitas – Roman, Wolf, even young Adolphe – that you don't find here... Their minds, of course – full of alien chaff, casting-offs and fancy dress...'

'You have a trouble bonding anywhere,' says Fulvio, stroking Mack's cheek, leaning over Sylvia's back ... she's bowed with the thought of Cook, he of the magic ladle, the devil's cauldron...

'Mack should be there, beside our special guys,' the head guy says. 'We've tasters, bonzes, everything you need to win an alien land. It's boundaries, of course – the more you want them, the less you like what you have got.'

★

Mack says to Sylvia, afterwards. 'This job, even with the fee – was Sophie's poisoned apple. Whatever I advise – the result is terrible... The place might disappear. Or like a mould, a jelly, grow – infest – a leprosy...'

'Nothing disappears,' says Sylvia. 'That's what they say. Metamorphosis. That's what we have inside, that's what we are. You might end up wise. A saviour ... a skin pinned on the door. It's you to choose – you take the first step, then – maybe there's a drop to nowhere, maybe an abandoned diamond cuts your sole... You're rich, or else you're jam...'

'Sophie – she wanted to see the shrine – it was just steps, up and up, and then no more,' says Mack. 'A door...'

'Next time, take the crowbar,' Sylvia says, pushing him away. He tries to walk with her into her room.

'It's all trangression, I suppose,' says Mack. 'This disposing of the lines, the people standing on them.'

'It's your mind, Mack,' Sylvia shouts through her locked door. 'That's all we have to go by. Usually, no one goes to places – we look at maps.'

'Sylvia, my impressions are the truth,' Mack shouts.

'The pigments are what's written on the tubes: they're true as goldilocks: it's the picture, Mack! True and false, or in-between – that's what's significant. Perhaps it's just a photo you coloured in, perhaps it's all weaved out of your head,' Sylvia shouts. 'Or clinkers in it, quite encysted. Go away!'

★

'You know what you should do,' Anouk tells him. 'You're not Candide – that garden's overgrown with weeds – abandon it... The rocks: there is your trail...'

'It isn't easy. That is not our side,' says Mack. 'Fear, empathy and reason – those must be added on. I'm in the wrong place, naturally...'

'Forget the right and wrong. Say what you think,' Anouk says.

'No,' says Mack, 'I'm corrupt. Fear has corrupted me – and caution too.'

'Well,' Anouk says, 'don't start your trek again. This time, you're motorless, you'll trudge along the track, and there's the shrine, the staircase, the iron door closed – besides, you don't believe in shrines, or memory, and ancestors, what you've been left: the chosen son.'

'I should withdraw,' says Mack. 'Take Adolphe. Anyone could have destroyed and hidden him – anyone, and stash him, live or dead – just anywhere. Me: or you, Anouk, or Master Wolf... Or Roman, come to that. All of us – responsible.'

'It wasn't me,' Anouk says. 'Though maybe I'm not convinced – where do I stand? Who knows what drives me on, or maybe I've a bad flower in my brain...'

'I'd let you off, Anouk, 'says Mack. 'Except it might increase my guilt ... my guilty thought. I should take up my architecture... Someone once said I had the gift...'

'It's not just building huts and towers,' says Anouk. 'It's fees and contracts – and you shape the people's lives, their work, the shade they stand in, – all things you don't imagine, Mack.'

'I feel a deep anxiety,' says Mack. 'Can it be love? Or maybe I took in a worm when we were sleeping in that place. Could be – the tequila...? It's true a building is the biggest thing you can produce. It forces on you, it's there where once a guy bodged brownish pants and sold them cheap; another stuck on rubber soles... Immense. Its shadow falls upon you, a copper's heavy hand... It's a nail, Anouk, unique. No one reads through a book, a symphony is incomprehensible. The whole of music, once cut out the words, allows no dance: you're pressed so tight, the most to do is wave your arms and sing along ... you must have learned the words before...'

'Perhaps it's love,' Anouk says. 'You're not trained for other things. Stop playing the reactionary! Anyway, you don't read books, and all that turgid stuff. Now, ask yourself – why can't you join the people we saw battling in the street? Doesn't it attract – guys wanting just a little more, for just a few of them? Is it their enthusiasm turns you off – maybe they've some cult you can't support, a religion unbelievable? Are they destined to embourgoise-ment, a version palid, kitsch, of those old guys in Paris, bustles, shiny hats, moustache wax, all that? Would their success, if they foresee what that entails, destroy the lustre of their wretchedness?'

'They are not me,' says Mack. 'I am not them. I back them from afar, and with reserve. Power, Anouk: that's the problem underlying it, that's my problem you won't grasp, that's my problem I can't grasp. You don't see my difficulty, I can't see a way out – I won't say an answer... No one has an answer, everybody wants to have a ride in it. What would Wolf do with all those hands? Make them mamluks, janissaries? Those black slave armies, marching to Baghdad, city of peace and greenery? Those hands... does he draw them, study them, prototyping for the robots that will mow his fields? And Adolphe... obeying orders, that's for sure, maybe some mental reservation, first, a private plot, staked out in his head, carnations and roses tended there amid the yellowing desolation. Then, his suggestion to the Master – impertinent and sharp. Enough for Master Wolf to know – "this guy is not for me, not on my side..." Someone is always found to do the dumping, cutting off the prints, then front and back legs, the head – its expression stuck between aghast, resigned, and irritated...'

'No one did that to Adolphe,' Anouk says: 'Adolphe was an eagle, up high, near the roof. You're not the enquiring sort, Mack. That's why you'll never be a president of anything. You don't see anything clear, that might show someone important in a lurid light. Making a judgement weighs on you, it blocks you, silences. Being judicious, getting it right, down the centre line. Reactionary – that's you; your problem too.'

'It isn't quite so, Anouk,' Mack says. 'Adolphe was an eagle, sure. Up near the roof. Like you, I saw the guys in wicker cages...'

*

'I have to renounce it, politics,' Mack tells Sophie. 'I am not prepared. I'm not convinced. Many things will be accomplished, "conquered" by the humans: time, distance, mortality. All that will be modified, reshaped, maybe understood. Conquest? Obviously not. There will be many victories proclaimed – but there's nothing there to win, nothing to resolve, no triumph, no finality: no revelations. No goal. Battles... Every war is civil war. On it goes.

'I must have a better theory. More study. A purer mind. Then – practice.'

'It's a big thing to say,' says Sophie, much disappointed. 'Especially as you see you'll fail. Are you sure you're up to it?'

★

'I set you up before,' says Sophie. 'Because I felt ashamed at how little you knew and understood. Now – this is the last time.'

Mack says, 'Everyone gets more than two rounds.'

She points her long quill nose at Mack.

'Don't stare,' she says: 'We know each other well. One more try. A banking friend...'

JIMENEZ: INVESTMENT BANKER

'You could act,' Jimenez says. 'Most people have to. It's not enough to strip now – the public answers back and criticises. You'd not face that. Boxing? You're too small. What's left?'

'I thought of something in command,' says Mack. 'Driving, diving, floating – in the desert, on sea, in space.'

'It isn't you,' Jimenez says. 'It's all fixed, the orders come...'

'It must be Fulvio,' says Mack, with some bitterness. 'I could free-flow ... Aurora...'

'Has a body up her sleeve,' Jimenez says. 'No one would peek at you, your billows, little dark places flashed...'

'What do you do, Jimenez? Do you hunt?' Mack asks.

'That's right, Mack,' Jimenez says. 'I judge. I don't give sentences – I throw you up, I stand aside as you're found inadequate, and spiral down, a dried-out pod... Of course, you may enter in the Spirit ... vindicate poor Sophie's choice...'

'I'm not in debt to Sophie,' Mack protests. 'Here we are, meeting on two river banks – you, safe over there, me, shouting across, an otter making a dam between us – it could be a bridge, or else...'

'Don't tread,' says Jimenez. 'Capital. I'm sure you have been told before – it never dies. It grows, it swells like the universe, indifferent – benevolent, if you think how it's still there, and could implode in density so tight – why, it would fit inside a vase, a shoebox – even a shoe, they say. The shoe of God.'

Mack urges him to reach the point: 'Capital – it never disappears,' Jimenez goes on. 'It passes through, metamorphises – in buildings and in cash, in songs and riffs and emeralds – you think you catch it – no! It's the abstract of abstractions. It may be bigger, even, than the universe, waiting to finance the next – evanescent, shimmering wings across the pool of space...'

'But,' Mack says. 'Buildings fall down, you lose your cash, the sure thing wobbles to the floor...'

'Capital,' Jimenez insists. 'Does not fall down, die, get beaten. It gives power – it fires the guys in hard hats, social classes, empires – those come and go – capital endures...'

'Me?' says Mack.

'I can give you access to it, Mack,' Jimenez says, wiping mud off his co-respondents' shoes, his linen pants. 'But the secret – one that everybody knows – I've told you first, so's you don't get attached to it – forget the idea you can possess a Capital. So, Mack, remember: on capital, you hitch a ride, a circuit on the roundabout. It is for fun.

Whatever use you make of it – it is a gift from God, a belly-laugh.'

'But the guys?' asks Mack. 'falling from heights, grown old and twisted? It's my fault...'

'Maybe it is,' says Jimenez. 'The universe, however, works like that. It's up to you: they'll bring you schemes of every kind. If you are true to Sophie, you will choose and follow through – the ones that bring you greatest joy.'

'Investment banking, Jimenez,' says Mack. 'Was it for this the species stood erect?'

'Imagination, Mack,' says Jimenez. 'Not book-keeping, not the belief that profit means you have a slab of capital, as though it were agate, chalcedony, perhaps.'

'Come over the river,' says Mack. 'So's we needn't shout.'

Jimenez is dapper. No one this century has been that. 'I stay on this bank,' he says. 'And I can't be arrested – if I came over, though – it is a different world.'

'That's a wonderful invention,' says Mack, amazed. 'Just that water, an otter, not even a beaver, can make a bridge, and on on side you're safe whatever you might do, and on the other...'

'Don't be a false naif,' Jimenez says. 'Getting to enjoy things isn't so simple, or you'd have done it sooner.'

*

He's right, Jimenez. Mack wonders what he's done, to need protection from arrest. It doesn't matter – he's safe, on that side...

'What does enjoyment mean, when you've access to capital?' asks Mack. 'Big goods? Big buildings? Ships? Big women? Big theft?'

'Lackeys all around?' asks Jimenez. 'You'd enjoy that? Incredible. I favour more the modes of the Escorial, Charles Quint. King Roger had it right... They'll come to you, I said: you follow up the one that tickles you – I told you, if it fails, capital grows just the same. Even in the same place. The first test – is to get out the office that they give you, out the door and out the building... You should have stuck with Sophie, Mack – she is the source. We get on fine...'

VIVIENNE

'What's your punishment?' the lady asks.

She could be his secretary – there's not a letter that he wants to write. 'Perhaps it's because I'm black,' says Mack.

The lady laughs – she isn't fun like Anouk, not at all, but tags along behind Mack, waiting for dictation, as if she's paid for it. 'People don't write letters now,' she says.

'What do we do, sat here, Vivienne?' Mack asks.

'Don't be so glum,' says Vivienne. 'You sit and eye my breasts. You don't do anything about it. It's not jail, nor attacking a city with a gun. You sit, and then the people gather, you bet on them, on anything, the rich and mostly poor. You do what you like with them, but it's best you ignore the lot, get them to work for you.'

'And then,' says Mack, 'I'll be out the office. You bet.'

'I know you think I'm a fluffhead,' says Vivienne, 'but it's just me, trying to cover up. My family was all killed in the war. Militia. I've nothing left.'

'That's terrible,' says Mack, embarrassed and backing off.

An office is a skinny room, dressed up, where these two persons sit and stare at one another, waiting for –

'A Mister Chagatai dropped in from Mongolia,' says Vivienne. 'He wants you to help him start a meditation centre and water park. I thought it was what you'd like. There'll be birds – cranes and divers.'

'Mongolia's full of those,' says Mack. 'Retreats,with statues. Only rich people would want another one of them.'

He thinks of Master Wolf's compound, and all the problems there.

'He's here!' says Vivienne.

Chagatai laughs a lot, like all Mongolians, and has blue tamgas tattooed on every finger.

'I want to visit the site now,' says Mack.

'It's not just where rich people can do drugs and launder money,' says Chagatai. 'Poor people will work there and sing, and do drugs, and make them too, and send cash though Western Union.'

'It sounds like what interests me,' says Mack, not having thought. 'But it needs doing bigger, or else you'll lose money. Think as big as you can.'

'Oh, I do,' says Chagatai. 'And you, Mack, just add anything you want – it's important to be big, so's we don't lose money.'

'I'm off, Vivienne,' says Mack. 'Do as you want, think big as you can. Here's the key.'

*

Chagatai and Mack – the talk's of camels: far across the steppe you see a row of brown furry knolls browsing – beyond, there's the beloved river. There's mention of a goose house – 'But, Chagatai,' says Mack. 'Where is the fun, the joy for me? It's you who will command, have the respect – or maybe not. But – I'll be looking for my fun elsewhere. The steppe will flower – I'll not be here...'

'You could learn to herd the camels,' says Chagatai, 'Milk them.'

'Meditation?' Mack asks.

'Or those long trumpets...' Chagatai goes on. 'Throat singing.'

'Wisdom,' says Mack. 'Like Sophie has, I want. What you suggest is farming.'

'When you meditate,' says Chagatai. 'You know where you want to go already. That isn't wisdom.'

'The children of the rich will come,' says Mack. 'Not the rich. They're always sad.'

'Like you, they wait,' says Chagatai. 'Chingiz – his children had the push but not the edge. But then – money isn't power – I have the power. I'll build – you'll just supply...'

'But I'm not rich,' says Mack. 'It comes from somewhere, probably screwed out of someone or inherited.'

'Then,' says Chagatai. 'Talking so – you don't know much about the riches or the power. Anyway – mine is art: and there's the tragedy. There goes life, "without rest, but limited in time" – and here's culture: once created, immutable but atemporal. You're stuck, Mack – not just with your limited life, but with the limit between your life and your creation.'

'I know,' says Mack. 'About the limits and the prisoners. And, since you bring it up – what did Chingiz want?'

'Not capital, for sure,' says Chagatai. 'He killed a stack of people. Cities too. In my part, the Indians came back and traded. Power? But there were his children, his death to come, erasing everything...'

'Power for ever,' Mack says. 'An illusion.'

'Not if you believe,' says Chagatai.'

'They say it was the climate drove them, that, and the technology. Ponies and archery. Civilisations to plunder. Talent and madness...' Mack can't imagine why, or how. *On s'engage...* Like everyone.

'The monks,' says Chagatai, shrugging, 'They sadden me. They've read those sacred texts a thousand times, and they value them, and stuff written down, it seems it holds a special knowledge, and the smartest kids come up and blow the trumpets, chant the words – but all they have, look forward to, is bits of down time, chatting, looking at mags, feeding the geese and getting presents.'

'I want knowledge too, Chagatai,' says Mack. 'If there's no wisdom to be had. I've nothing else. It's a present too, when it comes.'

'You have the power to give me cash,' says Chagatai. 'That will go on for ever, for as long as I'm aware. Children aren't interested in stuff immovable, they'd sell and flee.'

'You said it, Chagatai,' says Mack. 'You're building culture. They want flux, instead. That's the tragedy, they say. I don't see it as a sad tragedy, not like those dead, stacked up, the disembowelling.'

'Oh, that's a story,' says Chagatai.

'There's not much choice in the universe,' says Mack. 'Fun, wealth, and power. You have to love one or the other. I could stay here – watch capital, like clouds, waft across the sky, a *Windbeutel*. See the flowers come and go. Run the religious side. That would all make up knowledge, Chagatai.'

'You might look wise, but wise you wouldn't be,' says Chagatai. 'And you'd get in my way. Find another girlfriend, have her take you off some place.'

'I know it's rather trivial,' says Mack. 'Self-regarding, to think so much about your own potential, destiny...'

'Yes,' says Chagatai. 'It's trivial...'

'But, after all,' says Mack. 'Chingiz was just one man. Among a crowd, for sure. One destiny, you'd say. Shaping the base, deciding – East or West...'

They sit on stools, around there's nothing but low grass, the flat, the sun... 'There's no water here,' says Mack. 'No splashing birds...'

'Camel's milk,' says Chagatai. 'Is richer than the horses give ... Koumiss – that just takes out your wrinkles...'

They drink from shallow cups, not much like skull pans...

'Give me the money now,' says Chagatai. 'Forget the waterpark.'

'I could stay here, Chagatai, with you, my friend,' says Mack.

'I'd prefer the gold to yuan,' says Chagatai.

Two guys, sat here, who talk of destiny, of how to coax some wisdom from their knowledge, knowledge that grows with the setting sun, the west is glimmering off, Mack thinks, a new creative life will dawn – Aurora: she could be signed, sing her incantations as the tables spin, here there'd be Fulvio's gamblers, and me and Chagatai, taking our cut, the monks above ... everyone fired up...

'Camel urine's better still,' says Chagatai. 'The problem being, that it's hard to catch. It's that which fires you up, let's you ride tirelessly for days, straight as an arrow, making history along the way...'

Mack drowses on – he thinks how we could be in a movie, a *Secret History* of America, conquering the West with just a pistol and a fascist mind ... shares in Pony Express, naturally... Oh no! Mack leaps up – not a movie! –

not with one of Paco's endings, where we fight our
brothers, then it ends, no one is left but goodbye guys, all
sweaty males, no kids, with all those cadavers to pile or hide
... the West is won and lost at once, and so is all the rest ...
the East, no longer red, but golden, rays a-quiver, over-
arching, swallowed by aliens ... a dawning over ruined
walls.

'Peace, my friend,' says Chagatai. 'Tomorrow I shall
raise the central pole, and order decks of cards, and wheels
– for prayer, for luck, for monks and for the rest of us...'

Paco is far away. Chagatai pours from a flask – the
urine's rich, a blend of rye and myrtle. He and Mack sit on
through the dark.

★

They slump. The dawn is cold: Chagatai recites, '"The
world-revealing bowl, is – I myself". That's a consolation,
Mack.'

'It's thin,' says Mack, filling Chagatai's hands with
capital. 'Don't let it all fall down. Trust to luck and ten
percent...'

'That's old-time modesty,' says Chagatai. 'Ten's what
singers and strippers hope to get.'

'You're right, Chagatai,' says Mack. 'You've a billion
punters coming – a few will come rich, some will leave rich.
It's genius – it's the *Secret History* of everything...'

'Of course,' says Chagatai. 'Now, Mack, here's your
string of ponies. They'll take you to the railhead – the train
will pass – not at 3.10 maybe – there's snow drifts on the
line, and Yuma... Never heard of it! Maybe in
Manchuria...'

'I expect the Indians came from there,' says Mack, eager to be away.

★

'Well, Mack,' says Jimenez: 'It's all encapsulated. You've tied it all together – where can be next?'

'You're plumper, Jimenez,' says Mack. 'Sophie may be worried that your pump will seize...'

'Oh,' says Jimenez, stuffing neck-fat down inside his shirt: 'If you invest – it almost always goes like that, to fat. Sure, it's an intimation – but – your stock can fall, and then you'll need to feed on your accumulation ... Anyway, it isn't news to Sophie. She found you skeletal, Mack – lean as a bean. She knows you're a reactionary, Mack: Vivienne – thinks you're elitist too.'

'Mack!' shouts Vivienne. 'You smell of pee! And to think – I put my new clothes on, a welcome...'

Her sweater reads, 'Suck it and see'.

'I'm leaving right away,' says Mack.

Jimenez puts Chagatai's receipt – some scrawls on birchbark – in a safe. 'The lawyers'll sort it out,' he says. 'We're doing well. Dear Vivienne,' – he cuddles her – 'You stereotype her. She's your boss now, Mack... just like me.'

'That's good for her,' says Mack. 'It's all the same for me.'

★

'Chagatai was disappointing, in the end,' says Mack. 'Though knowledge seemed abundant, all in all, it was just power, without the fun.'

'For me, no disappointment' says Fulvio. 'Change comes from out his place: they don't believe in anything except themselves. No religion, no literacy, no cash. Just the drive, the movement, the rush. They're the next big thing, Mack. All the petty crap – about a stasis we could all enjoy, whittling jujus and message sticks outside our huts, jiggling puppets in religious wars – all that is swept away.'

'I just saw a casino on the steppe,' says Mack. 'Irremovable. Aurora says she won't do gigs – she says those wheels that click and whirr distract...'

*

'Here comes another scheme,' says Jimenez. 'Vivienne will introduce...'

'Mister Ji and Mister Amin: Mister Ravi something, Mister Anatoly,' Vivienne says, quite unimpressed. 'They know all about you, Mack.'

'Monkeys love power,' says Mister Ji.

'Camels – they go with wealth,' says Mister Amin – 'They're not rich themselves, in terms of the disposable, but they enable it.'

'Parrots love fun,' says Mister Ravi. 'Though it's not the kind you'd choose to share.'

'I rather disagree,' says Mister Anatoly. 'Monkeys love fun. I'd say they're wise – their brows ... the meditation, many seem bonzes... They all have just the knowledge that serves – though each is outwitted by some prankster, or some foe ... in every case, it's us. This consortium...'

'Wisdom is the recognition of one's limits,' says Amin, running a finger over the writing on Vivienne's chest. 'But that means knowledge and wisdom are forever in contrast. Knowledge knows you get eaten, wisdom is being resigned.'

'No!' says Mister Ji. 'Wisdom is being something else, so you avoid the fangs.'

'Fun,' says Anatoly. 'Is the answer to both those – both unattainable, but fun – you can be professional with that. Fun is the gateway to beauty.'

'That's true,' says Ravi. 'If you have fun, you must be wise not to be vulgar. It's a limit, too. But there's no limit to riches, whereas too much wisdom would be excess. Pompous – even ridiculous, a patriarchal ape, thinking he made the world because it's all there in his head.'

'Parrots and camels,' says Mister Ji. 'Hard to think they think they're powerful. I'm not sure about the parrots' fun – they seem frustrated, dissatisfied – you can't say that for camels, but it doesn't mean either kind has great things before them...'

'Hey,' says Mack. 'I'm not just into qualities. Give me some quantities, my friends!'

They're all round him, a jolly group – white shirts, white ties, nothing to fear from any one of them. No big luggage, little cases – in their heads is anything they want to know.

'You're problem is,' says Mack, 'you think one of these things – let's say power, riches – will lead to all the rest. It isn't so – it's like a game each knows from home: you choose a token, usually an animal, and round you go, each on their Ramayana. nothing you win leads to more wins, to something else, and you might say the game's to make the others lose.'

'We know all that,' says Ji. 'That's why we're here. Mack – you don't seem broken, even worn, and yet there is some weakness in you, some doubt – of no account, no relevance, something left to you from the past, a legacy, a history, descent or patrimony, family and legends – throw them away! Enough!' and laughing, they whirl him round, and

Ravi says, 'You are an architect – so, build! What if it all falls down – almost all always has! Some guy will have to prop it up or knock it down – it's quite irrelevant which way it goes – let it be beautiful and fun...' and so they prattle on, till Vivienne steps in and says,

'I've checked them out, these guys – between them all, they've not a qualification, a quality, between the four of them, their families disown, the cops – there is no claim...'

'Yes, yes,' shouts Anatoly, 'that is why we're here! We want some capital – if not from here, then somewhere else, we'll use it and then let it go – for sure it comes from people screwed, made destitute, ground down by making plastic things or trudging streets until their boots give up...'

'Mack!' Vivenne shouts. 'Go with them – and you're fired. I'll protect you, maybe, if you stay. What do these guys propose? Before you leave – you should find out!'

'Capital's a horse,' says Ravi. 'Wandering among the flowers. You ride it for a while – and then you fall – the horse goes on, and faster still without your weight...'

'You guys...?' asks Mack.

'A brilliant idea,' says Ji. 'A compound. Maybe a park, with birds and streams, some zebras too. A place for rich kids, relax – meditate, maybe blackjack: a throw of the dice...'

'And monks?' asks Mack.

'Oh, that is real genius,' Amin says. 'Maybe some Sufis – go well with the roulette wheels...'

'There was that nice Anouk... You try what you can't do, Mack. It's an obsession...' says Vivienne.

'You're all nice, Vivienne,' says Mack. 'That remains your stereotype, best hold on to it. Anouk's waiting for a prisoner, feeding the animals.'

'Waiting for prisoners, protesting, feeding the capital lest it runs off – that's our new role,' says Vivienne, quite content.

★

'This scheme of yours,' says Mack, as the five of them run laughing down the stairs – 'It's not the leading edge.'

4

JEAN GABIN'S DOG

'IF I COME with you guys,' says Mack, halting on the threshold. 'It will be like I'm dead. Remember, Gabin does his bit of acting and gets shot, then the dog runs off the ship, frantic to find him, but Jean is dead...'

'You've got it wrong,' says Ji. 'Gabin was not its master – the dog tagged along so long as it was fed. It had its choice – and a new search opens up before it...'

That quay – its fogs of war, fascism – Marseilles? – the gangsters come from the tempestuous isle, Corsica, the dogs of war...

'You're not quite dead, Mack,' Amin says. 'We should all die for something – even love. Sex and a document, maybe. If you're a dog – there's no shame there – enjoy it! There's nothing better than being what you are! Mind the traffic, that is all!'

'Accept it, Mack,' says Ravi. 'You're dead. And you're a dog that runs. You are our running dog, Ji knows about that.'

'Yes,' says Mack. 'I like that. Alive and dead. It's good. That's knowledge – behind that iron door, another stair, and then the panorama – flat, a river, dry in summer, frozen for the rest... Why, it's nearly wisdom...'

'Crap!' shouts Anatoly. 'There's no wisdom coming – you've got already all you'll ever have – what difference would it make if there was more? Another Vivienne, to throw you out the door? Another text to learn, another spin – you fall down dizzy – see! it's the universe that spins – away, away, anywhere – nothing's there...!'

'We don't want,' says Ji, 'to take a margin from the gamblers. Luck – is only a fortune by a play on words. Returns so mathematical – they've no attraction. So – I thought, let's make and sell antiquities, and beauties genuine – I thought of Gandhara. There's genuine and fake, if that makes any difference, excepting to the price. Or else there's Hellenistic. Bronzes – *cire perdu* – there's a challenge! African – the margin's higher, but there's others want a cut... Or – we might find Australians – originals – who'd work for us, and do some pieces, fantasy... The idea is: beauty's the gateway to riches...'

'No,' Ravi says. 'It's banal. There's no power – you're always waiting for the market – it drops the bottom from your genuine, and then the false attract the cops... Besides, there's the company ... those arrogant and ill-informed, making up the provenance, cheating on what's sold, the price... No, it's criminal, dear Ji, and either you get caught or else you end up as a dealer. What a fate!'

'No,' says Amin. 'It's not the selling, or the making – it's the buyers! Those fortunes! Big cash has no responsibility, we know – a dollar may do good or bad, but a billion ... it's like tumbleweed. It's true that beauty leads to fortunes – useless to pretend the other way around, that wealth can lead to beauty...'

'Then there's the people, wandering round...' says Mack. 'Buying the postcards...'

'Nothing is theirs!' shouts Ji. 'You can't unhook the stuff! There's guys in every corner, stopping you. Those frames – they're chastity protectors!'

'It's true,' says Mack: 'Consider. Is beauty big or small? Here today, tomorrow gone – where does it go, where does it die? If it's immortal – I resent, no, I hate it! I and my eyes – and ears – we're quite irrelevant. We humans – aren't involved. Birds in the sky – no fortunes there...'

'Rare ones, in cages, though...' says Amin.

'No, it's the sky,' says Mack. 'That is the nub...'

'The sky is always changing,' Ravi says. 'Besides – it's not immortal...'

'Five of us,' says Anatoly. 'Is one at least too many. Dumping each other – that's the point...'

'Forgery of documents, impersonation, fraud, assault, espionage, blasphemy: illegal entry and exit, breaches of public order ... and I don't know what else...' says Vivienne.

'Going where you want and being who you are,' says Anatoly.

'I denounce,' says Vivienne. 'That is my tic. It's stronger than I am. Pay no attention. Go with them, Mack.'

'She's good,' says Amin. 'No cash – but blessing. That's not bad. Of course, optimism is a wager. Night will fall – we see the signs of sunset, the sharp rays poking in our windows – Vivienne, she was unlucky – or her family was. Now – the camps, you wouldn't die in them, for sure, but you'd do anything not to end up in one.'

'Come on,' says Ravi, 'we're all businessmen, looking for the business that will make us something else. Rich, beautiful ... maybe we should try power?'

'Who would win?' asks Ji. 'If I ran for president – you know how it would end. Amin doesn't have a country, just the bits, held together by those armies and the cops. Ravi comes from the wrong area, it seems, the language and the faith don't fit... Anatoly – rather weedy. He won't convince.

That leaves Mack – he's weedy too, but in a most distinguished way. Maybe an empty place? Siberia?'

'So long as it's not another thing that I can't do,' says Mack. He wishes Anouk would be around, advising. Siberia ... the dawns are magnificent, the sunsets – death, the clock run down.

'Aurora could sing,' says Mack, jollying them up, all of them, those without future glory too. 'At the inauguration. She'd love that – the black cities standing in the white ... steam rising, soundless, ethereal.'

'Bring whoever you like,' says Ravi. 'Those women are all invisible.'

'Not invisible,' Mack says. 'Transparent. That's how I like people, people like you guys, a gang from vaudeville.'

It's time. Down the gangplank. There's no Master Wolf, no master at all. The dog is made to trot. It trots.

*

'You need a platform,' Amin says, 'and here's the train.'

'Everybody knows,' says Mack, 'that if the species carries on, it needs spirits, zest, maybe some cornichons, some curly peppers, like Pan's horns... Everybody knows – you need so much, a tot, to live on, so much time to meditate: everybody needs exactly what you need to keep yourself alive. We all know that. Propose it – they think you're crazy. Equality? No one will vote for you, even if their cash is hanging on the tree... That's what I stand for. Otherwise – the species goes extinct, it shrivels... Maybe that is not so bad, except it brings the other species down...'

'Yes!' says Ji. 'That inspires! That's the oldtime – the oldtime socialism we loved and lost!'

'I could save you,' says Mack, 'all of you, but you won't listen, you won't share, cooperate, stop beating up on everyone, each other. I'm right. And if you're right, that means you're good: at least somewhat.'

'No, Mack,' says Amin. 'You're not good, not good at all. Better if you ran back up the gangplank, put your head into the collar, sailed off – not Venezuela ... better shipwreck, an island where there's only other runaways, other dogs like you. You know what's good – but you – you are untrustworthy.'

The train stops. The cities are grey and lemon, vein ducts of black. 'Where's Amin?' asks Ji, taking out a wooden pipe, one hole.

'He's off, looking for bliny,' Ravi says.

'He oughtn't,' says Ji. 'They're forbidden,' and he blows – a silence ... but the train starts off – there's the taiga, then the tundra...

'Only the train guard hears,' says Ji. 'It's painless. That way – we are four. Amin's retired. Now, Mack – refine your message...'

'From each, to each – I don't remember,' Mack cogitates. 'It's not that. Each has the same needs, like tigers in the wild... Jackals ... the same reward, and no regrets. Ji! We ought not deal with Amin so – this is maybe a quite hostile place...'

'No harm will come to him,' says Ji. 'He knows he should keep quiet. It's not like Wolf's little place – a midden with a single cock. One foxy type breaks in – and all is change and squawk.'

'Oh Ji,' says Anatoly, 'you do exaggerate! It's useless, doing what Anouk does – waiting for her bird to fly, perch on her shoulder ... and Adolphe does it all again, to someone else – like Master Wolf had done. She'll grow old so. Wolf is a primitive, like the master, Chad's Hissein Habré: – nails, wooden sticks, and plastic whips: those leave a mark. The modern way's with words, with lawyers even ... and to speed it up, with water. Electricity. Those don't leave a mark outside, they're cheap and clean, no one feels remorse for that, leaving no mark, getting the info like it's on a screen.'

'You must be clear,' says Ji. 'Mack, you are the Kaiser of Atlantis, of this grey and green expanse... No one should despair, no one eat someone else: it's you decides. You who punishes...'

'Yes,' says Mack, 'I know. It's in the interest of all. But being Kaiser – maybe that's the tricky part...'

'Then work it out!' shouts Ravi. 'You've time upon the train. Don't be a Candide, wringing your hands, letting it all slide. Speak to the people – here's the deck for orators...' and he shows Mack the little dais, back of the last carriage, where at every halt you can address the crowd, explain what species, species being, means.

'Bring enlightenment,' says Ji. 'Remember – most birds aren't netted, most aren't caged. They live out short lives, and sing. How they sing! Fear? Machismo? Property? You can change all that. The light, Mack! That's what you bring. Of course, when you're the boss – you must be feared. Spin out your theme from that...'

'From what might happen to Amin,' Mack starts. 'I stand aside...'

'Nothing,' says Ji. 'That is the point. He wanted something – he got naught. That's your lesson – stay away from zeros and the negative. Amin's a good guy – but his share would be too much, reduce ours to the limit...'

'Limits,' says Mack. 'How I know those!'

The inaudible whistle stops and starts the train – faster, deeper it goes on.

'Reindeer!' shouts Mack.

'Mines,' says Ji. 'Ravi, Anatoly – they say that too.'

'See them running ... roaming as they've always done,' Mack says.

'You're an adolescent, Mack,' says Ji. 'Men kill the reindeer. That is how they live.'

'Reindeer are a species; mines,' says Mack. 'Are holes. Holes kill the men.'

'Maybe in those holes there's elves and dwarves,' says Ji, and laughs.

'No – those are the men,' says Mack. 'That's how they go.'

'Out there,' says Ji. 'There's many angry men, they have their schemes, their angry families too – anger they cling to, not to you, not you as boss, and not your schemes. What will you do?'

'I'll ask you, Ji,' says Mack, unconvinced. 'What's next.'

'If we'd have made a liberation, I'd have gone with you,' says Ji. 'We didn't get the cash – so, now, for us – it's mines.'

'It wasn't up to Vivienne,' says Mack. 'She dreams that capital can be her private park, the shrubs in golden pots, the leaves in filigree, a hologram, some banker's monicker. You – like her – don't understand... You build, make debts – it's then they have to let you into capital. You think – it's them. Like, if I had the power – that's when the money flows...'

'That isn't wisdom, Mack,' says Ji. 'It's investment spiel. Wisdom flies in at dusk, when you can't see, on dark matt wings. For us, you too, it's back to digging holes.'

'It's true, Sophie's elusive, Ji,' says Mack. 'Bad-tempered and intolerant. But she's wise – if you follow her...'

'You end up here,' says Ji. He pushes Mack, and Mack clings on, the train moves slow, determined, though. If only he'd Anouk with him, Mack thinks, the two of them could overpower the rest, stay on the train – boffing Ji in his silver suit, the weedy Anatoly, Ravi in his ducks... All struggle, they move on.

Mack drops on the tracks.

★

Gabin's dog – it doesn't get a credit, but like Paco, trots to the next movie set – always the same role. That French army – never got to Venezuela, never read the history and deserted to a man and dog...

Mack stands, injured, in the taiga – of course! – he and his one-time friends, they should have made a deal with Chagatai! Just over there! You don't think, as you're rolling among the sleepers...

★

The Russians left definitive books: on war, the psyche. France – of course – left conversation. Friends. The English – manners, slowly getting worse – so what? He thinks, smarting from the fall, everything there was to know was set out years ago. So what, indeed.

Mack's a dog, without a book, nothing to consult, nothing to take inspiration from, now Ji's gone on ahead.

Still, he's a porous nose for storylines.

'Goddam you, Vivienne,' he thinks. 'Your greed, your parsimony. The militia didn't spot you, underneath the bed – amateurs, never finish their unspeakable job...'

★

'You'll find it hard, Mack,' Sophie says. 'To stop being a reactionary. You must try. Break out. Everybody does, who sees the rain that falls, the rivers run. It all flows, Mack. Conservatives seek a tranquillity – but they're always hooking on to some disaster. Everything is always new, dear Mack. Night will fall: there's light and dark – you can't choose to have all bright, all dull.'

'It isn't so,' says Mack. 'Up in the north ... eternal black gives way to endless light... Or so it seems.'

'Exactly so,' says Sophie. 'Don't be taken in. But don't exaggerate your doubts – you were on that committee, and couldn't make up your mind. A dog's heart...! Was it Sylvia behind all that? Another risky war in view? Master Wolf – back him, or dump him? Or a judicious censuring?'

'Oh,' says Mack, embarrassed, 'I'd almost forgotten about Sylvia. Fulvio talked about some atom bombs, some scenario extreme ... friends borrowing some...'

'Don't drivel, Mack,' Sophie says. 'You don't need convince anyone of anything. Fulvio kept a book; therein were his prayers.'

'You too,' says Mack. 'Sophie. Maybe I've put unfounded trust in you. All I've got from you – is falling off a train. Wisdom – maybe you have it – you for sure don't pass it on.'

'It's not a mortadella, Mack,' she says. 'I don't slice bits off.'

★

Anouk. She had a mission, everybody else has lives, they put them on like underpants and fart around in them all day. As for Sophie – the day they saw the shrine – that argument defined. If she is wise, thinks Mack, maybe wisdom isn't worth the pain of acquisition – and, what do you do with it? Sophie – she bums around talking superior – 'Don't be reactionary, sexist, but don't chance your arm, don't leap, don't look, write nothing down, don't hope and don't despair.'

★

'Anouk,' he shouts. She's waiting for Adolphe. The wall is high, but you can hear them, prisoners, squawking in their cages. The water pots are dry – maybe you should buy a lime, throw it over to them, maybe it will arrive sliced through the bars.

'That guy has limes, Mack,' says Anouk. 'Don't buy them, they're as sour as kingdom come...'

'Oh no!' says Mack, 'that kingdom. Isn't that jihad? They made us say it at the school – the punishments come before the crimes, the guys omniscient peek in your dirty mind...'

'Master Wolf gets paid,' says Anouk, 'by you, your friends, to lock guys up. Wolf's friends and enemies – you don't want them where you are: maybe they lie and steal. Maybe that's what I like in them... Wolf's strong, crownstone in the arch: his kingdom's king. He falls – and all the other guys whose lines are drawn to hold him in – they fall as well. His mercenaries, and his cash, his friends, the little book he makes you read and memorise – if he goes down, there's wars and penury that never end.'

'Anouk!' says Mack. 'I know you wait for Adolphe thinking he is innocent...'

'Grow up, my dear,' says Anouk. 'If he's innocent today, tomorrow, if he isn't dead, he'll ride his horse through waves of blood. And if he's dead – his horse will gallop through a tide of lymph and marrow, pus and brain...'

'That's terrible, Anouk,' says Mack, disoriented.

'I wait, that's all,' Anouk says. 'Adolphe may not be released. If he is – he'll stand against the tide, be swept away, or picked up by some pirate ship – and then it's vengeance. Or – war against each. Who knows? They say that shows us we are free. We're meant to be those animals that love and purr, and give our food to needy ones of other species swinging on another branch... Altruism, Mack, not scavenging.'

'The cash,' says Mack, 'we sent. Our group – had hoped by that to soften up the Master.'

'You don't want him soft,' Anouk says. 'That cash goes into cages anyway... Adolphe – he fancied me. I shan't forget, whatever else he does: – that's fortune, Mack. You don't forget. I bet if someone ever fancied you, you'd say they fit your values, how they show you there's a bower somewhere, where you can live for ever and be bathed in milk...'

'I need someone accompanying me, Anouk,' says Mack. 'Not representing anything, not with a map...'

'Oh, I've only constancy,' Anouk says. 'I don't make claims on how things might turn out.'

'The guys in cages,' asks Mack. 'How do they get on?'

'Everything adapts,' Anouk says. 'You know how disagreeable caged birds can get? Well, the guys squat, of course. They walk, of course – to fly, you'd need a great long court, like they use for pétanque, or that tough Mexican game – winner takes loser, you remember... They sing, of course. They say birds know each other by the smell – of course, they all look identical. But – when you're used to it, dear Mack, you grow attached to bars. The cage is cramping, but it's safe. There's food. It's hot – but that's for everyone.'

'How will Adolphe come out, Anouk?'

'Oh, maybe they'll just get tired of him,' she says.

'But vengeance? Resentment?' Mack asks.

'When they're out, you see they haven't flown – and now, their wings don't carry them,' she says.

'Adolphe?' Mack asks. 'I understand about a friend who's then turned into a bad friend: the anger felt's the greater than if they started as an enemy.'

'They're not the same,' Anouk agrees. 'A bad friend's lodged inside you, encapsulated – you might cut them out and put them in a jar, then find they've grown again inside. An enemy's no more than what it says. Ji – when he's boss up in Siberia – he'll welcome you. You thought you were his enemy – he pushed you off the train. But – that was that. You start again. Another match.'

'*Tlachtli*!' Mack says. 'That's the game they played. Quite like the game with baskets on your arm, the high-up ring – maybe from Haiti. Or Cayenne...*Pelote* – is that it? They borrowed it, and modified...'

'I don't like chance,' Anouk says. 'Game or not.'

'Oh no,' says Mack. 'It's sport. You need another quality – I don't have it, but you can win a series, over and over. Not chance.'

'That's worse,' she says. 'It's what Wolf has. What Adolphe wants. On and on – they're on the winning edge.

To you the outcome seems like chance ... but really it is something else, not what you find in history. Maybe in mathematics, there encysted from the start.'

'Wolf won't last,' says Mack. 'No one does. He'll even go to court, to jail...'

'Then – that won't be Wolf,' Anouk says. 'He's what he is when doing what he does – not being reprimanded. Anyway – everyone has cages. They can't think of a better way, a way to hear the songs, larks and vultures, each dawn and every dusk.'

'If you come with me, Anouk,' says Mack. 'You must tell me why you're leaving Adolphe.'

'Oh,' says Anouk, 'I'm not leaving him. I'm just not sitting here outside the jail.'

'What do you see in him?' Mack asks her.

'He's ambiguous, that's what,' says Anouk. 'Maybe he'll never be released, nor die. Maybe he'll come out a liberal. A liberator. Or nothing. Or a warrior, an executioner. If you speak with him, there is no clue...'

'He seemed passive,' says Mack. 'But that means nothing. What's right for here? A soldier? Lawyer? There's courses you can take to be both those.'

'Try to be metaphysical,' says Anouk. 'It might suit. Think of me as Mona Lisa – the pic's not her, but really someone else or nobody, lots of trial sketches underneath, and many many copies... The version on display – that's the puzzle; not the woman. Not the face. Besides, who's interested in what's hanging up? The show? Three arty guys...'

'I'm interested,' Mack says. 'Though not much. No question – so no answer. And it's Adolphe hanging up, not you...'

'Exactly so,' says Anouk. 'But he's flesh. Cramped and twisted... I'm normal, I'm just painted on.'

'Come away, come away, Anouk,' says Mack. 'There's nothing you can do here. We know the problems, the answers, and not doing, not being able to do, a thing... We've all been taught – love is the answer, then there is morality... We all agree on everything... Those cages – they could be put down on the ground instead of hanging, tilting...'

'Oh,' says Anouk. 'There's rats. And damp.'

'We had to read,' says Mack, 'about the spiritual, and the Untergang. Decline of civilisation. And of course – the collective subject, oily from its factory job. Out of that, we have a clear vision of where Master Wolf belongs. There's no problem – he's been classified.'

'I had time to read as well,' says Anouk. 'Sitting here, under the tree ... the blue birds ... and the monkeys. There was peace, except, of course ... you know ... the absence.'

'You understand why people turn to music,' Mack says. 'Play loud, and flash the lights. And yet, I don't think Adolphe is the answer – not to anything. He seems a cypher.'

'He's my cypher,' Anouk says. 'But what's the difference, if I'm sitting in the chair or gallivanting round with you?'

'This is the place,' says Mack, 'where Aurora could sing by night.'

'No, Mack!' says Anouk. 'They sleep. And, forget Aurora, all these people you can't catch with your net. You are a solipsist, Mack, there's nothing to be done with you. You think there is a centre in the universe – it isn't so; it isn't you. Everything is busy, travelling out quick, into new nothingness. Maybe we should go to Brazil – it's full of people indeterminate...'

BRAZIL

The news comes: Adolphe twisted free one of his bars, garotted a guard ... the keys lifted ... is on the lam!

'I don't believe it,' Anouk says. 'Mack – have you got the tickets? Does Vivienne still send you cash?'

'Oh yes,' says Mack. 'I'm still her tout.'

'Now, don't begrudge,' says Anouk, buying furs and thongs. 'Her card is useful, leaves no print. We're off!'

When they land, Anouk says. 'No nonsense. Here, love is consummated, love and much beside. Be prepared, Mack, no twittering about invisible brown birds.'

'What's a link between love and consummation, Anouk?' Mack asks.

'I meant we're here. Brazil, not Paris,' Anouk says.

'You're thinking about Adolphe still,' says Mack. 'Adolphe's a heavy name, dragging a heavy story, too. And do you speak the language here?'

'I don't know,' Anouk says. 'What language is it? I don't speak any language...'

'We have to find our way,' says Mack, 'if we can't speak...'

'We'll speak,' Anouk says. 'We shan't write poetry, but we can hum.'

'That way, we'll only meet with foreigners,' says Mack, wondering if Ji or Fulvio has a network here.

'Almost everyone is foreigners,' Anouk says. 'I've mastered almost everything – it's like the other places,' and she gives money to people around, so they smile and nod.

'Some things work everywhere,' Mack says. 'Maths. Reason. Gravity – they work. Vivienne's card, though, doesn't.'

'I can't read these signs,' says Anouk, kicking at the cash machine. 'Do you eat the things there's pictures of?'

'Don't eat anything, Anouk,' says Mack. 'I'm sure they're like us, but I can't grasp a sense. The alphabet's one that I'm not used to.'

'They let us in,' says Anouk. 'But that's the start. How'd we know if our opinions conform to theirs? Are you a communist, Mack? What kind? A heretic? Religious freak? Romantic fantasist? If you've religion, you've kept quiet about what kind – I've never seen you pray, or sing a hymn...'

'It's useless trying to decide what you believe until you know what's banned,' says Mack. 'We have to find some work – the only signs for that I know are slicing sausages and digging holes – neither of those is what I want.'

'That cash I gave away,' says Anouk. 'For good will – maybe I could beg it back.'

'It might work that way here, Anouk,' says Mack. 'It's worth a try.'

'Don't panic, Mack,' Anouk says. 'They'll think we're speaking in tongues, have us locked up.'

'Maybe that's the safest thing,' says Mack. 'We'll play insane, learn some words and talk ourselves outside and cured...'

'No, no,' says Anouk. 'That's not the life I want. Who knows what madness theory they have here...? The knife?

The pill? Or even worse – the talk... Which we won't understand. They'll think we're dumb.'

'Try pointing up, Anouk,' says Mack. 'They'll think we've fallen off the moon.'

'Mack! Don't despair,' says Anouk. 'If love is consummated here ... I'll offer mine. Not say a word.'

'It's true,' says Mack, 'I won't need vocabulary to be a pimp – I could get by... But – there's the competition, and the cops. Words count.'

'I'm ready for the sacrifice,' says Anouk, 'but I don't want you as my pimp: the sex is not the sacrifice: it's keeping you is not the life I want.'

'For sure, this is Brazil,' says Mack, calming down. 'There is the statue on the hill, the people wearing flimsy clothes, the dance, the tumbledowns, the luxury... There'll be the Indians up north: for us, it's worse: they'll speak at least two languages that have no sense...'

'There'll be some learned guys who've spoken for the first time with some Indians...' Anouk objects. 'No one has a language readymade for coping in that fix.'

'You know by instinct what an Indian does,' says Mack. 'You know too what they were. They all remember water – the crossing, ice – back there, gone eternally, the beloved river ... Amur! The tigers and the cranes... They carry tools, they paint themselves, they're angry for the future, but... They're stuck here, in the dwindling woods... Guys like us, Anouk – we give no clues. No bow, no tattoo, sceptics for the future, ambiguous as regards the past... We send no message. We are laminate, Anouk, we're chipboard silhouettes.'

'We should despair,' says Anouk. 'We fall, there's nothing stops us, ever.'

'There's bound to be a net, a network that will catch us,' says Mack. 'A restaurant you order food by numbers – I could be a waiter there. Traffic! – parrots, trees – passed from the forest to a boat, sailors vowed to silence, pain of death, pain of existence. Ji – would have a net. Fulvio, another... They would catch us, bear us up. Give credit.'

'Don't let's fall among your fucking friends,' shouts Anouk. 'The best would be – if Paco makes a scary movie, I could be the star...'

'Calm!' says Mack. 'Look – those kids, like bonzes, deep into their paperbags – they're Ukrainians. They won't speak to me, maybe our colour puts them off. A sniff of their glue, Anouk, should be enough: cadge, and sleep. Tomorrow we can learn some words – tonight is not a life choice... Imagine we're Kierkegaard, locked in his freedom, conversing solo with the imperious void. Inventing top gods, then kneeling, crawling before them. No sentences required.'

'I don't understand you, Mack,' says Anouk. 'I'm glad for that. If you're the only person in the world I could talk to, and yours the only language, it would be ... diabolic. "Only youuuuu" says the song – terrible. True love grasping everything! Leave me alone! Better no one than the brute beloved. Best – just "love": the goal.' She keens: 'Sing, sad bird. No words, no history, no territory that anyone would want...'

'Some criminals are bound to pick us up,' says Mack. 'They'll give us work – we've nothing they can steal.'

'Rich people live like this,' says Anouk. 'They have others who carry dirty coins and notes for them. They long to get away, have solitude without the justifications and the arguments. Silence – it costs, Mack. Most people can't afford.'

They sleep. It's cold. The next day is the same. It's hot. They smell. The people they don't understand stay further off.

'These buildings,' Mack wonders, 'what do they do in there? Fast food? Exotic dance? It's all the same to us. Ministers. Who needs their ministry? See the traffic – going from there to here and back again.'

This is what there is behind the iron plate, when you have climbed the stairs, this is the shrine, he thinks; it's me and Anouk, standing there, eyes whitened from the blackness. Speak! A babble. Or a word.

★

'It's right,' says Anouk. 'They said this was a new world. It will have a new language. We shall explore beyond our death. Can't speak – can't think – you're decomposed. The Indians here don't understand Mongolian. It's what they lost. It's better so. They must learn to speak with all the people here. Maybe we, Mack, you and I, will learn some words – enough to labour, to sell our muscle-power, to slice, to dig ... whatever they don't want to do, we'll do. In silence.'

'You're right, Anouk,' says Mack. 'It is the land beyond our death. Nothing before has any use. I think I've picked out rhythms in the speech, inflections – but, of course, no sense.'

'You travel, Mack,' Anouk says. 'You bump along with all kinds – and you're indifferent. They dance, they sing, they plan conquests, they steal – they dig up jungles. What I want,' she says, leaning so close he sees some secret teeth, the ones that do the heavy work, 'is to see good. And evil.

But now we're impotent and blind, here in a place where we don't understand the language...'

'Does good and evil need a language?' Mack asks her. 'Why me? In your scheme, what do I do? Does anybody count? Why good and evil?'

'Everybody has a project,' Anouk says. 'The good and evil project is the top! Nothing is more human. All the rest is twiddling; indifferent stuff. Who cares if cadmium is found on Venus, if there's a tiny particle with legs, if in a hundred years we'll all be living for another hundred years? It's all four-colour maps and artificial viruses. A dictionary of what there is, a crossword-puzzlebook – there's not one sentence in all of that; no jug of words that makes you think, or bristle with enjoyment. I told you "why you" Mack. Your lack of qualities is a lubricant. You make us slide. As for language – it shouldn't be essential, shouldn't underlie, define, the good and evil: – that way, you might think by changing what you say, you change the categories, even, you can make them void.

'And, Mack! If we can't find good and evil here, where we don't understand a word – what kind of place is this? Evil must be everywhere: and good as well, or else we'd live complacent lives without them, in a place they don't exist. But – such a place ... you think you'd find the city, or the desert, where it's all hohum – but each twist shows there is something large and masked behind it all, that twisting knife..'

She asks, 'Do you find them, good and evil, in degrees? Or should we look in absolutes?'

'When you've located them, what then, Anouk?' asks Mack. 'You're satisfied? They're there, just like you thought. Or do you look inside us all, us people?'

'Oh Mack,' says Anouk. 'When they're found, I will tell you. It's so big a quest – maybe it's foolish from the start.'

'It seems you're an explorer, Anouk,' Mack says. 'You don't hold a brief for good or evil: for, against: just want to put them on a map...'

'Someone will see us, Mack,' says Anouk. 'Right now, speaking of maps, we are a telltale blank. A nothing in the sea, the blue. Under this palm tree, in our ragged clothes, a message but no bottle for it... Someone will come and rescue us. This is just a conversation, Mack: humanity, good and evil – I don't take sides.'

'Tell me Adolphe doesn't come into this – pure, treacherous, his toxic "love..."' Mack says.

'I don't think love has to much to do with this,' says Anouk.

'We could starve to death, if we don't find the words,' says Mack.

'They're much more advanced, the people here,' Anouk says. 'For us, it seems the question's "trees or savannah"; it's "eat-eat-eat" all the time, and battles if we can't. They're peaceful here, thinking of more refined, more complicated things.'

Mack agrees. 'But perhaps quite inconclusive, no more focussed and definitive than us...'

'You make me feel quite infantile,' says Anouk. 'Good and bad. Adolphe in his cage or on the run. I hope at least they're gentle with him, when he's caught. Give him a trial, at least.'

'I insist,' says Mack. 'It's not a bad place here – no one at all is hurting us, trying to do us down. Our needs ... they are not satisfied, but not because there's malice here... They're too refined for that.'

He shows Anouk some cloths. 'See! The people here – they don't throw things away. They're clean. But – these are dirty ponchos that I found. Crawl inside one, and we'll hunker down...'

There's steps up to another building, they can't work out what it's for – perhaps some need they've not yet felt. They lie. Embraced.

'Maybe they will put us in a show,' says Anouk. 'That way, we would be fed.'

'Who knows what animals they keep, out in the forest, or in cages underground?' asks Mack. 'It's us who could be food!... What's bad, Anouk, is not you didn't find your good, your evil. You've found no love. That's what you think you want.'

'There's no way out,' says Anouk. 'We can't even do like Adolphe – kill someone and run. Found better worlds.'

'There's no call to be reactionary, Anouk. We're stuck here, that is all,' says Mack. 'Guys here have taken leaps ahead, we can't communicate. Do they love, and are they happy? Do they care about all that? My old revolutionary...'

'We can't get out, Mack,' Anouk says. 'It seems this is our end, our casual fate, fighting for nothing. Just a sentence. Something that makes its point. Your old revolutionary...'

DIRECTOR'S CUT

'I've finished all those movies,' Paco says. 'Started off a whole bunch more. Better than a restoration is the remake from within, new ends and new beginnings. Aurora – I've in mind for you, in my new tale, a speaking role...'

'Oh no!' Aurora says. 'My voice is like a crow's!'

'That's what I want,' says Paco. 'When I dictate the words, you rasp. Be yourself – just trill and improvise.'

'It could just be me, of course,' Aurora says, and preens. 'Silence, good looks. It's called a portrait. Hang me. Come and look. I must be paid, of course.'

'There's Mack, Anouk; they're back from making money in Brazil,' Paco says. 'I can't use the faces, naturally. Their voices – they are beautiful. The rest is ugly. Besides – I need offload my debts on them. Maybe they could do a movie without views, without the visual?'

'That's called a book,' Aurora says, quite angry now. 'A portrait and a book – that's quite enough from you. Those are stuck where you've laid them up or down.'

'Strange,' Paco says. 'In the poem, it says, "your nightingales live on: death, the ever-present thief, steals everything, but not the songs..." Maybe because they're volatilised already. You know, Aurora, you think the movies move. They don't: they too are hung upon the wall, the heroes jiggle up and down, like in a shadow play, they're ghosts, more real than you or I, but still like marionettes. They can't get out the door. They're stuck, Aurora. Now, you know what moves?'

'Money,' Aurora says. 'That is my hope. My wish.'

'Debt, Aurora,' Paco says. 'That's where the future lies. That is tomorrow. Poverty today, riches ... to come. That is the revolution. Debt is the rocket, fires us from our planet misery on to planet doubt. Uncertainty. That's the only remedy – that is the cure for death. Not life after: life now!'

'Windows and doors, Paco,' Aurora says. 'I've always stayed outside – is that a help?'

'Debt is air, Aurora,' Paco says. 'It bears up the birds, it seeps in everywhere. In or out – it's all the same. Air – rots the kings, queens and knaves, eats the saints and martyrs in their tomb, blows down the posters in the heavenly square, degrades the flags until they're rags, draws lines upon your face and thins your hair. Air!'

*

'Paco!' says Mack. 'Ask anything, but not for cash. Vivienne – in her jealousy – she's cut me off...'

'Debt, Paco,' Anouk says. 'That will see you through. Do something magnificent – a film on Adolphe's place. He's part of me – his life, so terrible...'

'He should be terrible too,' says Paco. 'That might just interest me...'

'Oh,' Anouk says, 'there'll be a war. Crowd scenes, Paco, bangs – all stuff you never did before...'

'Of course I did, you innocents, trembling like mice before the python's gorge,' he says. 'We lost some boatloads doing river scenes – *The African Queen*, I think it was. A bore. There's Fulvio, his group ... who's side do they promote? Follow the money, Mack, big bets show the way!'

'Those groups,' Anouk says. 'Experts, committees. They precipitate it all. All sides want to pre-empt their choice, or cuddle up to them. Then countries follow on, take their soldiers out the box...'

'Both sides, Anouk – not "all",' says Paco. 'Keep the tale simple: one on one. Look, when I'm in charge, you give the answer quick and clean.'

'The fault is Mack's,' says Anouk. 'The greater fault is Vivienne's. It's those two, upset the balances.'

'There is no balance, Anouk. You are wrong,' says Mack. 'Your quest for good and bad – the question's rigged. You set it up so's an answer will be found, it has to be, because your terms are pre-defined.'

'I'm right, Mack,' Anouk says. 'You're wrong.'

'Excellent,' says Paco on his toes. 'I see a story – all it needs is someone who will write it down for me.'

'Mack's a sceptic,' Anouk says, rearing up. 'That's the worst kind of infidel. You slide about like curds...'

'And you're a bigot, Anouk,' Mack shouts. 'You've no substance, you believe in symbols.'

'I believe in Adolphe,' Anouk says. 'Love has no symbols...'

'It's stuffed with them,' says Mack. 'And your adhesion to that tortured creep – does it do you credit? Where'll he run to, making friends with who knows who? Maybe he'll get religion, then get bombed. Maybe his new friends will push him into war...'

'Go to, go to,' laughs Paco. 'Out with the poison rings, the stabbing in the alleyway – that's where the poetry springs out. Don't shout – just do! Forget the drama and the camera – real blood looks much more fake than on the stage...'

He spins on his heel, like the guy who no one knows his name. 'I love you, you two crazies, Mack who thinks he's sharp, and Anouk who thinks she's hard... I've been to the top. Big countries, who know your destiny, have it all on tape. You know, they say the implants in you – the teeth, the eyes, the veins, the other stuff, your wooden leg – they say the aliens put them there. Instead – it's them! Big countries! They know exactly where you are, where you hide your cash, and where you hide the books – Tough Boys' Bumper Album 1930. Materialism and Empirio-criticism – it's all the same. They know. Poor Adolphe – he'll run, make a heap of friends – give them the faith, materialism, who knows what – and guns maybe – then comes the bang!! All is resolved. Poor Anouk! And poor Mack – looking for wisdom, beauty, love – even a spot of truth... You idiots! But – what a movie you'll all make!'

★

'Sex first,' says Sylvia. 'Entertainment after.'

'I liked it better when you had those dogs,' says Mack.

'Naughty boy!' says Sylvia. 'No wonder Vivienne cut off your credit!'

'Why'd she do that?' asks Mack. 'I understand business, shuffling the papers. No mess, no dross.'

'She knows the truth about you, Mack,' says Sylvia. 'You faithless pilgrim! Who'd trust you? I don't. You make things easy – Vivienne's jealous. You're good with capital – it's people let you down. Sophie was too retro, the beautiful Aurora's dumb as stones. Plain Anouk – talks of the good, but won't give you love. Nor wisdom. What's the good or bad in that?'

'You can be witty, Sylvia,' says Mack. 'Should we make a fuss? About that country and its prisoners?'

'Oh, prisoners,' laughs Sylvia. 'Do you really care? If you'd had a religious youth, you'd know about all the prisons you'll be in. Now – enjoy yourself –'

She calls it 'swimming in the lake' – you don't get wet. Then there's driving blind along the coast road – you don't fall in the sea – you sweat.

'In my travels,' Mack tells her. 'There's Indians everywhere. Some with blue eyes, red hair. I'm one, Sylvia. We were in Brazil – didn't understand a word. A waste of time. Wastes everywhere – flattened, covered over. Unfinished buildings – why did they start them?'

'You know, Mack, how I want revenge,' says Sylvia. 'Where there's people angry, like me – it's better not to rile them up. I'd like to, naturally: forks in the eyes! Maybe, though – crossing the border. Incursions, Mack. Excursions, not lawyers, don't you think?'

'A little homeland war, Sylvia?' Mack asks. 'Is it wise?'

'Well,' she laughs some more, 'it won't be beautiful, for sure. Sort it all out. You won't need tip your hand. Advantages for everyone – including history,' she says.

'No,' says Mack, 'I won't go.'

'My little war?' asks Sylvia, nipping him quite hard.

'The empress lost hers, Sylvia. Really, is love for your man at the bottom of it all?' he asks.

'You haven't understood,' she says. 'Patriotic wars show who's really on what's side. It makes things clear. And clean.'

'Sylvia, it isn't so,' says Mack, not convinced. 'Guys are so complicated. If it's Adolphe ... he's in Anouk's territory. All of him. Border provinces – they don't come in.'

'Fulvio,' says Sylvia, ignoring him, 'Is out of gladstone bags and into high finance. He wagers on the stuff that looks like clay. No doubt you find it everywhere around. There's always desperate guys who'll dig it up. If not – there's sheds that's full of uniforms...'

'This is trite stuff, Sylvia,' says Mack. 'There's more to things than you imply.'

'Of course,' says Sylvia. 'On our way, there's stairs to climb, there's panoramas, guides to pay, those foreign sicknesses to suffer – maybe you will die from them... Remember, Mack, you're in the soup. You're in the stew. You float around – in there, there swims a bone – tough, eternal, very savoury. Climb on to that, poor Mack, maybe that will save you from the cycle: eat, break down, eliminate.'

'That image, Sylvia... disgusts,' says Mack. 'There's piles of bones around, you want to add another heap...'

She leans back: the rocky divan ... rocks all around. 'You've been buying, Sylvia,' says Mack, nosing into closets. 'Those birds – they're stuffed?'

'Clockwork,' she says. 'The latest shout! The dogs – you'd have to oil them, take them out, or else they rust.'

'It's a nice thought, birds.' says Mack says. 'Human. It means you're permanent. And if they were electric, you'd need wires – so naff!'

The birds sing the bulbul song. 'It makes me cry,' says Sylvia. 'That's good.'

She looks big, on the small divan. 'I have everything in hand,' she says, pushing Mack towards the door. 'I tell the bigger bosses what they want to hear – it's what I want. I can be prudent – they can not. They matter – I'm the source. Without me, no river, and no flood.'

'Last time we were away,' says Mack. 'We didn't understand a word. Next time – suppose we're blind? You want to get your way – suppose we can't see where ours lies? Suppose we're deaf...'

'You want so many shapeless things,' she says. 'I tell the truth. Truth used to be desirable. I only keep a tiny piece of it for me – the rest, I told you, Mack... You should know everything – but you don't count! You're always right, behind the ball – but no one cares! That's the lesson, Mack: omniscient and impotent, a stupid God, a protestant, too human!'

She winds up the birds again – how many of them there are – of course, you don't need food or space, they wait for you to wind up their eternal spring... You buy the eggs, until the store runs out, or you get bored... There's hundreds in the cage, all silent till the mood takes, and you remember where you left the key...

'Think, Mack,' says Sylvia. 'Truth is a nightingale you have to wind...'

*

'Sylvia's right,' says Fulvio, handing Mack controls of a tough game. 'Wolf needs more food – best take it from those clowns beyond the hill...'

'I never thought I'd have to go this far,' says Mack, pressing buttons, lose their heads. 'The group – I thought we were so wise. We'd recommend incursions...?'

'We're in emergency,' says Fulvio, driving a fierce motor down a mined highway. 'Wisdom's not sentimentality, you know. Countries is the old way. You can't keep people locked in them – they need to roam, be nomads if they can – look for the right stuff – rivers and grass... Can't sit in shacks and read those magazines...'

Fulvio avoids an ambush, swims a stream, knocks out Mack's tank. 'You haven't got the hang of this, my friend,' he says. 'You need quick hands. Think Liszt! Only an octave, but cascades; a wonder. I regret not being in the gaming game right now – everyone a winner! – if you lost, there's a next time, not like life: and fellowship as well. In business, now – you don't get criticised, it's not like politics – people praise you: and when you fail, they're glad.'

'You like strong countries, Fulvio,' says Mack. 'It's laws you don't – they help people you don't love.'

'Look out! There, Mack!' says Fulvio. 'You've lost your last two squaddies. I've been on the run myself, until they put me in the group. You have to find out who's on your side – anyone who's not should find their place elsewhere. There's lots of room still – being a pioneer gives satisfaction, Mack – you need to read the books...'

'Are you being wise, Fulvio?' Mack asks, throwing his joystick angrily on the floor. 'Sophie – she thought it was wise – or it might make me wise – to give me the responsibility. I wonder – what exactly was the purpose, and for who...'

'This is your problem, Mack,' says Fulvio. 'We have to sort things out – I told you, it's emergency.'

In the street, there's an old Charger – beneath its purple overcoat you see the old lizard green and orange flames. Fulvio waves Mack into the hotseat. 'No,' says Mack. 'I don't want this. I know it is the real ... I hear it. It's like us killing all the birds, *but* – here comes Aurora.'

'We killed the birds – *and* here comes Aurora,' Fulvio says. 'Come on. Things follow things, they don't compensate each other. This is how we are. There's no way out – the only question is, how fast, how slow. Climb on the car. Show me what you can do – there've made a special track...'

'There's so much we can do...' says Mack.

'Oh,' Fulvio says. 'It's being done! It's all too late – we know everything about ourselves – our loves, our character, the figures that we draw, our figures cast in shadows on the walls the Titans built, the sacrifices, massacres, the altruistic suicides. Sense and reason, love, disgust – it's all been parsed, dissected. The only thing we don't quite know is how our illness ticks, when each will exit, leave the scene; how many times be saved, and then dropped in the firepit, or ground up to manure the vines... When we know how sickness works, that's the last thing. All we need do is wait, suffer the false alarms, and then... That's why, Mack, you must drive this fucking car along the track, outwit the foes, the mines, the birds disguised as fighter jets, or do you think it's the reverse?... and on and on, with whoop and wave... We've found ourselves, Mack, explored our every crack and wrinkle: we're curious, we picked at everything until we'd unravelled it, and that's us done and finished, each in their tiny theatre, playing the play and then to make the last bow, naked before no one, no public, wondering why there's no one there, each off naked in their theatre...'

'There's no little theatres, Fulvio,' says Mack. 'It's stadia, the colosseum without the savage beasts.'

'Get in the motor, Mack,' shouts Fulvio, 'Show you're one of us.'

They hum along – Mack turns into bear, then wolf. 'It's hard to steer with paws,' say Mack – and Fulvio shouts, 'There's two guys on bikes behind – they must be cops, swerve and ditch them, they are CRS, the best there is...' The cops fall off. 'Not in the ditch,' shouts Fulvio. 'Keep to the hardtop. The gulley's full of dynamite,' and up they go and down, and Fulvio glues the pedal to the steel. 'Out!' he cries, and Mack's a swan, Fulvio clings on – it's swan's way, now, and Fulvio says, 'Mack, you must win the war – Groucho knew – it's done with the moustache, or the toupé: Baffone knew it, you should try a full Zapata...' and Mack looks down – there's a glass sheet, the Charger's gone right through, shards like a necklace – a lovely reef, a greenery of buttock shapes with nipple sprouts. 'Those are the other motors, Mack,' says Fulvio. 'Now the oiltrap's been laid out for the next crew.'

'It was so beautiful,' says Mack, 'The horse, the Charger. All metal –' and they hear the tape, playing along, heavier than that the metal doesn't come, it sinks the car – but they soar up, 'It was so beautiful!' says Mack.

'Oh Mack!' says Fulvio, 'Don't be a fuddy-duddy – now you're a swan, you're monogamous, your bride will age with you, become a gummy crone, bent double, leant on her washing stick...'

'No, no,' says Mack, his wings creaking in the storm. 'I'd prefer a series of young sprigs, who're fascinated by me till they dump me, and leave me with our ugly chicks...'

'Don't miss your legend, Mack,' says Fulvio, riding along, now grasping Mack's soft white back and digging in some claws. 'You could have your genie make you into an eternal boy, a ten-year old... Not your fancy? Back in the bottle with him, quick, they're tricky guys – another wish? That you would always win, and nothing ever change, of course!' But naturally, they can't change anything: there's bottles like a carpet on the ground, all full of genies, hundreds, maybe more, with fishing rods and blunderbusses, trying to bring the valiant couple down – until...

'You lost, Mack,' Fulvio says. 'It could be that they rigged the game! I've done the same myself. Another time – we'll do the magic trip, the poetry, of wandering in the forest, striding to the savannah, then we'll copulate like apes with all the starry crowd, a set big as the Sahara, a movie with everybody, all in gowns and trews. Desirable? Wow, Mack! Your parts will go redhot...'

'Fulvio,' says Mack. 'You'd need an eagle, not a swan...'

'Oh dear,' says Fulvio, setting up more games, 'I hope you've stamina. Fascism flies! The rest – took off, short flights. That's it. An interim. Everyone is feisty now, they see the last few years are filled with eternity, shafts of gas like pikestaffs rise from the cities, rise above the dust... Magnificent! But, Mack – beware! The old pawns – they ran off – over the field, the hedge – and now they're queens!

You can't rumbust about – there's others too. Prudence,
Mack! Stick to your quest ... but keep some other goals,
close to your chest...'

'I need some cash,' says Mack. 'To buy some guys...'

'In that place?' asks Fulvio. 'I'm not a happy man, you
know.'

'Why should you be?' asks Mack.

'I was born there, Mack,' says Fulvio. 'They're goodtime guys, every one, despite the darkness there. I know
them, every one, winners, losers, guys who'll sell you blood
– is it theirs? A dog? An enemy? Best take it, Mack, and pay
– wherever it comes from, it's hard earned...'

'Oh,' says Mack. 'Of course – you are the expert. I
wasn't born anywhere of use. And – I have to pay the guys,
I know – you need do that everywhere...'

'The richer someone is,' says Fulvio. 'The more you
need to pay. Of course, an empire costs a patrimony – a
country ... you can fit the necessary inside a gladstone bag.'

'I don't know whose side we'll end up on,' says Mack.
'And I'm not cynical like you. There's always good and
worse – you just need to be an expert to decide.'

'I'm an expert,' Fulvio says. 'I know you all. And you're
an expert too.'

*

'Don't spend this money on yourself,' says Vivienne. 'And
not on bad things, do you hear?'

'You're strict,' says Mack. 'You cut us off when we were
in need.'

'Oh Mack,' says Vivienne, caressing him. 'There's rules.
There's intuition too. You know, I collect ... just little
things. So little – it's my fancy, they have broken off

another world. Don't you agree – there must be other worlds, this one's such an imperfect one, it must have been a reject, or it's trying to emulate some model somewhere we can't see... These little, tiny things – maybe they're part of something so immense we can't make out its shape...'

'I've heard that, Vivenne... Don't! You're crushing me...' shouts Mack.

'So big,' says Vivienne, tightening her hold. 'So tiny I can hardly see...'

'You're right,' says Mack. 'Nothing can be so insignificant, or so big it doesn't want to communicate. I'm sure they speak, your collection, beyond this world – maybe the language, too difficult for us, when we were there...'

'Yes,' says Vivienne. 'People in forests that's so large they're designed for quite another place. And people you don't know where they're from... They've fallen off, it's clear...'

'Oh no,' says Mack, 'I've been where they came from... it's quite flat, you couldn't fall, you're carried in the spate down to the sea. You end up as naked Indians.'

'In coracles,' says Vivienne, 'spinning like cogs. Those days – the light was brighter, dazzling; and the dark – like it had never known the sun.'

'A place beyond,' says Mack. 'They say there's always light somewhere that you can see – even in a gladstone bag...'

'No,' says Vivienne. 'I collect, so I should know. Light takes years to come to you. If you're born before – you are a baby from the dark, the black. There's heat, no light. No language, Mack – in the dark there's only grunts...'

'Let me go, Vivienne,' says Mack. 'And see it for myself.'

'You are an innocent,' says Vivienne, tongue in his ear. 'Like those who I collect.'

'Just give me the card, the icon, or the figurine,' says Mack, quite frantic. 'So I can access the capital...'

'You struggle, Mack – what is it that you have to lose? All's gain – like it or not. I'll give you something that you've never had...' she says – waving a capriccio with her hands.

'What is capital, Vivienne?' Mack asks, struggling, 'Light or dark?'

'What's the colour inside your head, Mack?' she asks. 'What colour's thoughts? Brain – you never even feel it, but it thinks, invents oxygen and rays. Music – has no emotion, yet it's full of it. How come?'

'There's something beyond colour, Vivienne,' he says, fighting free. 'It's clear. And beyond language too.'

'Oh,' she laughs, 'so, you're a mystic, Mack?'

'Give me the key, Vivienne, so's I can get the cash,' says Mack.

It's small, white metal. 'And the lock?' he asks.

'The key,' she says. 'That's what you asked for.'

'There was once a door,' says Mack, 'but not connected with the place ... where I need cash.'

'Behind the door?' she asks.

'How can I know?' he asks. 'The top. Of something. Anything.'

'Well,' she says, 'you don't need cash for that, nor yet a key.'

'Fuck it, Vivienne,' he says, 'I'm not a mystic to that degree.'

'What's the money for?' she asks. 'Unlock the cages? That way you need a key. Beware – those flighty things – they peck. Some you know are moribund, some, that they're dead. In any case – they've lost the power of flight. What then? What can you buy? An army? A cause? A religion? Like yours – a cult of personality?' she laughs. 'Expansion? Security? A guerilla?'

'With enough cash – all of those,' he says, anxious to flee. 'Everybody with a key is trying every strategy.'

'It's true,' she says. 'In every head there is no light or dark. Its colourless – soundless too, I bet.'

Vivienne hands him the key, returns to her magazine. 'Kilos lighter, darker hair...' it says.

'Watch out, Mack,' she says. 'There's much much worse than nothing.'

'Yes, that's the fear,' says Mack, running down an everest of stairs, out in the dusky light.

*

Your cruel and treacherous lover, Adolphe,' Mack tells Anouk. 'No recognises him today. No one reads the book, no one looks into his cage. He took flight? Killed? Flew his coop? Was executed? – we shall see. When Sophie said I knew as much about that place as anyone – I thought that she was right. Like they say, they're goodtime guys – they don't know how to suffer... There's no direction. It all turns into its opposite. What's your attraction to Adolphe? You want to be betrayed? Or enjoy some ambiguity? Your Adolphe – he's a victim, then a corpse: or else transformed: the iron will, the boss.'

'People think it's about Hitler, you cretin,' Anouk says to Mack. 'You know, how people take on these names – it could be Adolphe Sax – or Hitler's grandfather. The Adolphe in the book – he killed for love. Just one. He made the mould – how far can you go, they love you, you urge them to their deaths. Goes well with Wolfgang – the only

Mozart anybody knows. Playing along together, improvising. The cruel lover, sour – and the sweet...'

'You could make a monster out of them, Adolphe and Wolfgang.' says Mack. 'A golem. Solder them together – right and wrong, left and right, executioner-cadaver. Adolphe will burst forth – vengeance! "More rigour, discipline – send them to the fields, have them eat grass."'

'If you've the cash, Mack, you can do anything,' Anouk says. 'I don't want a part of it – not you, not lovers, not bosses – and no music. Adolphe's poor lover – "you'll let me languish, weeping, make me die at your feet ... my suffering haunts you" ... and all you want is that I leave you. How politick that sounds: beware Adolphe, Mack. They promise you the revolution, then can't stand the sight of you – unless you cheer them on.'

'We have to go,' says Mack. 'We can't get cash here – there, we pay them and take a cut. They need the food, Anouk – best have them take it from the neighbours. One or other leading, maybe both of them, Adolphe and Wolf. Patriotism's a wonderful invention, Anouk, so long as you don't fall into step. I don't propose acceptance, Anouk: just wait, distrust, plan – await your moment...'

'I'll say this to him, Anouk,' Mack says. '*Look, Wolf – you've problems, your people too. Unrest, hunger, your repression. Don't break laws, of course – but if you cross your limit, limes, we'd help you with the territory, deal with the diplomacy, all that. You must be humane, when the fighting's done – let out the prisoners...*'

'*Of course I shall,*' says Wolf. '*I might seem harsh, you don't know how dangerous and cunning they all are... Putting them in cages makes them feistier...*'

'That's crazy, Mack,' Anouk says. 'It's like: "yes, the French, the Russian revolutions – they're too good to miss. Just make a few adjustments, everyone's a fan…"'

'It's what one says, Anouk,' says Mack. 'You push the button down the road, using your nose. In your head, there's something big – colourless, of course: so big – you can't tell, from looking at the skull, how immense it is. It's like our capital – bigger than all the clouds, you enter with this little key… Those misty bricks – that's history, Anouk. What Wolf does – is what he'll do. Adolphe – a monster, probably: that's in the book. Still – I have the key right here.'

She laughs. 'Is there a lock? Do you know where the key fits, dear Mack?'

'It's not a thing you know,' he says. 'It's what you'll do.'

'Well, Mack,' she says. 'What can you do? Their will, that's all. Your mafia friend, Fulvio: you're in his bag. The others: Ji and Chagatai. You think you've made them, shaped them – it's quite the opposite, poor Mack. They're chancers. You're kept, Mack: all of them, from Sylvia to the bosses high above, they keep you. They don't even need to feed you. Until the cash arrives, and you can lick their hands – you'd only bark and whine. That's what you do – sometimes you run ahead, sometimes you tug behind – you're always on their leash. That is "your side": their heel.'

'I know all that,' Mack says, subdued. 'I can change it all.'

'No, Mack,' Anouk says, 'this is the wisdom. This is how it is. You know, and you can't do – that's what Sophie says.'

'Adolphe's the son of Wolf,' says Mack. 'What do you say to that, Anouk?'

'Love, Mack,' Anouk says. 'I've offered it. It bandages all wounds. But, it doesn't work, it doesn't stick where you would like it to. It doesn't do what people say it should.'

'People here throw stones at Wolf's bold soldiers. And – they want the edible grass that kills their farms. They'd back Adolphe in a revolution – but they're glad he's strung up somewhere, or on the run. They love their neighbours – cousins. They'd kill them all and cheer as they parade the victory,' says Mack. 'Where's the end of the rope that disentangles this?'

'Everyone is right, Mack,' Anouk says. 'Assume that: help everyone. You can't go wrong.'

'My hopes are wearing out,' says Mack.

'Your conscience, Mack – you should have switched it on more often, see if it still worked,' says Anouk. 'Your civilisation died a while back – it was just the stucco moulding on the castle wall. That old "good" and "bad" – it's dead.'

'I know the people like bad people,' Mack says. 'They call them strong or dedicated. Then, if other people are bad – not stealing things, but being bad all day, well into dark – they can be good themselves. Or victims too. If you don't like bad guys – you end up underneath them. Under the heel. Or else indifferent. That's what Sophie said...'

'No, Mack,' says Anouk, 'she didn't. She didn't have much to say at all. Of course, like me, you can try to love. They say "men love the good". I'm a woman – I don't, not especially. I don't think about it.'

'We could steal the money, though,' says Mack. 'We don't know who to give it to. We trust ourselves, Anouk – that's halfway to deserving it.'

★

Wolf's behind a wall – you think it's him. It could be anyone. 'You mean,' says the voice: 'I take the province next to me, you give me cash, applaud... Where's your conscience?'

'Oh well,' says Mack, 'you get the food, the river too – guys paying tax...'

'They're not rebels, though,' says Wolf.

'They will be, when you bomb,' says Mack. 'Of course, all this is new. History has changed.'

'I'm not sure it's changed,' says Wolf. 'But the presentation has. And I release the bad guys, have them run around...'

'It's your big chance,' says Mack. 'You're not Wolf, you're sweet Wolfgang. And bad Adolphe, the cruel lover – he'll give interviews.'

Everybody wins, everybody's friends.

*

'I can't stand,' Adolphe says, 'But you can kiss my hands. Bend down, Anouk.'

5

ADOLPHE

E HAS TINY FEATHERED shoulder blades...
'Pick me up,' he tells Anouk. There's a
harness, he could be a leather bag – his feet
curled like a concubine's, the claws a torment,
growing upward, piercing the flesh – a bag, striated from
the bars, a brown bird once alive, the black pupils ringed
with white, a clown's, a tumbler's. 'Swing me,' he says, 'like
a bell, a lantern,' so she does – there's no sound, but there
is a candlelight, it startles, does not illuminate. Anouk
swings him to and fro, he shits on her shoe, and she goes
on. It's love, her love, bigger than the word she hasn't
coined.

'I see a light,' says Mack, 'The papagayo's eye – all the
evil since the dinosaurs is there. How they must have
croaked and roared – their world ended, their gods useless,
exposed as fraud: down the creation comes – a bang: into
the caves, see the scaly mushrooms block the entrances.
The huge beasts – feeding on each other – does the father's,
mother's flesh – does it taste like chicken, raptors' taste like
quails'? Curse of the cursed lizards, the eyes bequeathed,
turn to the purity of coal: the green of everything, the
leaves, the grass, turned black. The red – passes into grey,
our brain. Passed down ... life, of course, our life – the red
blood goes to grey, a million years without the sun, the grey
passed on as brains, grey thought, the brooding on

144

apocalypse, the long primeval, the primevil – the long lurk. The aftermath, we clever monkeys scheming a fresh destruction, more perfect than the first.

'Now, throw me,' Adolphe shouts. 'Swing, throw, like bowling...' and she rolls him. 'Fuck you, Anouk,' he shouts, 'Aloft! I'll fly.'

She weeps. Maybe once – up in his cage, the wind that dandles him, he's flown – through the bars, like a sliced egg – over the wall – a thistledown, a tumbleweed, a burning bush... Here he is, the rebel, the eagle, replete with sucked out offal from Prometheus: would fly! would fly! And falls, rolls in the dust.

He's a ball of feathers, heavy as lead. 'Don't kick me,' Adolphe shouts. 'In the air, let me fly...' He raves. His crooked claws, nothing to clasp, 'No feet,' he shouts. 'Look at me! Nothing beautiful in me... I'm scrag...' Oh, his poor claws, penetrate his feet, legacy of those splintered perches, excema on his neck, the belly rounded as a rubber ball – the empty seed and water pots. 'No football,' he repeats. 'Throw me in the air...' a game, a sacrificial *pelote,* through the ring, the massive court, a *tlachtli.* A volador – the winged warriors leaping down, the pole-top spins – it seems they are in flight – all ends in sacrifice, a human going gladly, out into the warm air. A warrior's sport... They swing him to and fro...

'Let me go,' he shouts. 'Over the mountains, the river...' Vengeance. Or mission.

'We have to straighten Adolphe out,' Anouk says, wiping her shoe on her pant leg. 'Everything brings luck, they say – but he must stand up straight – and point. That Lenin's finger pose – how it inspires!'

'Yes,' Mack says, 'but he must be post-proletarian. But what? Prometheus? Liquid programmer? A giant, a transvestite dwarf?'

'Oh no,' says Anouk, giggling, 'we must forget the fashion – this Adolphe's for the future, with the cruelty blanched out. No more psychology, no more the bourgeois maschiliste. Constant's Adolphe – he'll be over, forgotten...'

'No hospital,' groans Adolphe. 'Other tortures I resist...'

'For love,' says Anouk. 'You must bear a little torment, dear...'

They heat up the tequila, lay him in the bath. The steam's inspiring when inhaled – you could write poetry, leant over him – 'Loosens you up', says the publicity – and it does.

'Speak! For the people!' Mack declares, twangling poor Adolphe's vocal chords, a bent twig thrust well down.

'For what you'll do, dear Adolphe,' Anouk says. 'You'll not need this –' and from between his chickeny thighs she twists out his tiny flaccid spout...

'Wait, Anouk: freedom, equality – it's true, those are debased coins,' says Mack. 'And – love's a nymph more cautious than in bourgeois times – but still... Adolphe's a potential hero. He may bring resistance, and, who knows – free trade. A bill of rights...'

'The cash,' says Anouk. 'Do we keep it? Or let Wolf and him joust, and winner take the lot? Food, water, arms – the people rushing to and fro and digging holes, and crouching in...!'

'Stop!' shouts Adolphe, waggling his toes. 'Wolf is not Mozart, and his gang – is gangs of wolves! Don't be taken in – those cuirassiers at the door, the white-gloves hanging round with booze, the inkstands silver-gilt – it's flummery, dear Mack. It's not like that! He's vicious rubbish, dear Anouk. I'll not disappoint, I'll lead the best, despite the odds, against the sods whose machinations led us to this point – my flag...'

'It's true,' says Mack. 'He'll need a flag. What will he write on it? What history?'

'Something with feathers?' Anouk asks. 'Look! His are coming off – what beauties! What a waste...'

They're pure as coal, they have the iridescence... Maybe it's the limes...

'Why'd they do it?' Anouk asks. 'The torture. It can't be fun for long.'

'Good guys pretend,' says Mack. 'It's for the info, though they've more than they can read. The bad guys – it's to show. Not reform, just extra punishment...'

'Five minutes torture – or five years in jail?' Adolphe asks. 'Which would you prefer. We're all sons and daughters here – the homeland. Brothers and sisters, gone to bad. First, you are reduced, and then you're killed. Why leave you lingering?'

'You were kept, Adolphe,' Anouk says. 'They must have thought you useful. What, to deter? For bargaining?'

'Oh no,' says Adolphe. 'That would be too smart. I died. It's obvious. I died, I was a bird – I flew. At last... The sun, the desert. Carrion. What joy! A feast! Those crumbs in jail – it's deprivation at its worst...'

'It's a conundrum,' Anouk says. 'If you're not Adolphe, you're still you. I'll call you Adolphe – that will do. We've resurrected you – after, you're never quite the same. My cruel lover? Or transformed, born from a shining egg, charismatic, polished up ... blown through...?'

'Yes,' Adolphe says. 'That will do well.'

'We must do history on you,' says Anouk. 'That may help us with the flag. Partition? Like Poland? That leaves headaches. War and breaking empires? You need a Grosz for that. This is a nation, here, Adolphe. Guys would like to keep those – they are things with borders, with a *limes* – so, it simplifies. Religion? – no one can handle that. It's murky water. Have you the faith, Adolphe? Is that the sparkle in your eye?'

'He's kept those birdeyes, Anouk,' Mack says. 'See – the pupils – they can spot the carrion from mountain tops. Adolphe's cleverer than all of us, more devious, maybe... Sylvia wanted vengeance, Fulvio a clear run for cash... That's simple. Religion crosses everything, it's a flood...'

'Rhetoric, Mack,' says Anouk. 'Religions aren't about the arcana, they're resemblances – they're distant cousins, well-known strangers you can't stand. They steal your legacy, cock farded snooks, keep your kids down...'

'Flames,' Mack says. 'That's how it ends. Cruel lovers drop through the stage, down into hell. The devil takes you if you don't believe. Born wrong – what can you do?'

'That isn't it,' says Adolphe. 'Here, we all believe the same.'

'There's too much detail coming out, Adolphe. Give us a line,' says Mack. 'An explosion – limited: a crisis someone can resolve. Victory! A helmsman, a nostromo who will pilot through the storm...'

'Oh Adolphe,' Anouk says. 'I loved you so – at least, the person that you were. Don't let me down. See – the danger for us all – the goal is riches, but you feel the flames – under the stage, and not just you, it opens, and we all go down... No betrayal, Adolphe, please...!'

'Be sure, if I can, I will,' says Adolphe. 'That's what it's all about, Anouk.'

'Maybe the answer's in the grass,' Mack says. 'Solves everything.'

'I'll bring all you guys in, and bring you down if so I must,' says Adolphe. 'Right is right.'

'Maybe we should take the cash,' says Anouk. 'Use it to find a place...'

'Now he's normal size,' says Mack, 'we can't get him back into the cage.'

*

'I hope Mack does the right thing,' Fulvio tells Sylvia, 'and takes the money. Rich countries, especially if they've had an empire – they love those smaller countries – they treat them like they treated colonies. They make them fight, corrupt them; love, hate, and dump their bosses. Mack deserves the cash as much as anyone. Capital – it doesn't drift and land where there are poor guys. So, let Wolf's tip stay in Mack's gladstone, or in Anouk's shoe.'

'More dogs,' says Sylvia. 'That's what I need. Three small ones – that might replace two larger ones, I think.'

'The more details, the less complicated it becomes,' says Fulvio. 'You start off with rich and poor – that fades away. They aren't in the mechanism. You're left with what I say, friends or foes. It works out as it must. People fuss, yet, they do exactly what they'll do. It works out as it must.'

'*Amor-dolor?*' says Sylvia. 'You're wrong, Fulvio. What works things out is interests: – it isn't interesting. You need a show. The stuff of life, Fulvio. Or else it's only graft and coffins.'

'You and I,' says Fulvio, 'you could teach me again how to do the tango. Or – we could go up the Rhine in a steamboat. There could be a terrible fire aboard – I might

save you at the cost of my life... Tell me, Sylvia – why did
they boil your partner?'

'Oh,' Sylvia says, 'he asked for it. But the pain's the
same.'

'It seems a curious thing to ask for,' Fulvio says, his
interest fully snagged. 'That's what I mean about
international things – the motivation's odd until you know
it, then it's childishly simple.'

'Children aren't simple,' Sylvia says. 'They can't
communicate, that's all. Their brains are scrambled at that
age. Then time intervenes, and everything is different, more
settled – in the medium term.'

'It must have been difficult putting up with him,' says
Fulvio, 'but I'm glad you told me – I hope it doesn't hurt.'

'It's the only thing that lobsters know, after all,' says
Sylvia. 'The hurt...'

'Let's try those steps again,' says Fulvio. 'Cut a rug.'

'You have to keep low,' says Sylvia. 'Like Astaire, low on
the ground. You go quicker – it looks like, anyway – you
don't clatter. You glide. The woman's higher off the floor,
just hooks on to you, slower and elevated.'

They try. She hums the melody. They teeter.

'Don't think you can bring those dogs into my new
motorcar,' says Fulvio. 'It's a Challenger. Dogs don't go
with that – maybe a big thin one...'

'Afghans,' says Sylvia, starting to cry. 'Don't do that with
your hands, Fulvio.'

WAR – THE MOVIE

'You mean,' says Paco, 'you've given that crook Wolf the stuff to win the war of annexation? Then he's humane? Your friend? The good guys will be hung up high, and everyone eats grass?'

'Yes, Paco, that is it,' says Fulvio. 'Of course, you make the movie freely. It will serve to keep Wolf quiet, and we're the innocents whose help and goodwill somehow has gone astray...'

'Oh, leave that out!' says Paco. 'I don't go near explosives! I'm just the guy who cleans it up – the story's told: the truth – a mote up in the sky, gyring, flapping in its vector – seeking the carrion far below, stretched out from drought and trophy hunts...'

'What can I be?' Aurora asks. 'A mother? I'm too young. Louise Michel? I'm best at scenes that titillate, an intimacy that overleaps the *limes*, far beyond philosophy...'

*

Here we are, in history, Mack and Anouk think. This is not for me. I wish I were not here, but know not where I'd be, or if it would be me. This isn't loneliness, being alone, this is what I am. I should have friends, who take me to another place and have me do what I can do.

The hut's the same as the earlier time. It smells of absent things. Whatever's been brought in, has been consumed here – people too, a quick encounter and no lingering. Two borrowed chairs, so Mack leans on the back of one, then moves around between them. A half-bath, borrowed too. The floor – a plywood sheet: it says 'A gift...' The light comes through the door, but there's a curtain there, and dogs and things like dogs twitch back the cloth – if they are cops, the light this brings is not what you would want.

But – the floor... No cooking's been done here, no fire. You have to heat tequila up outside, around the back, in an old twenty-litre tomato can: you need the earth to hold the fire. The hut – it could have been a library without a book, a grievance place for standing people.

'Standing people,' Mack says. 'You could put a plinth here, a head upon it. No marble locally – maybe basalt? Earth? Or wood and feathers. They'd come to see it: the struggles – they go on. This reminds us of the species. The head is not political – we are. Its thoughts – not ours, but thoughts still – we don't have to share. This connects us – it is deep and superficial. You could do without it – it seems a stone head's more significant than ours. It isn't so. Neither is...'

'If it's well done, scary, a chrism, a mystery,' Anouk says, 'it's us. Our deal with Adolphe – we are right ... a path...'

'Of course,' says Mack. 'Here – put Vivienne's draft safe in your shoe.'

*

'An art gallery?' Adolphe says. 'What a strange idea. Here in the village jail...'

'They say that art is of the right,' says Mack. 'Instead – it's the part of us that recognises – being the critical critics after gardening. Species recognition – the past encysted in the now.'

'Fishing and hunting?' Adolphe says. 'It's what the fiscals do, and special agents... Now – the cash.'

'Results first,' Anouk says. 'Payment after. On the stump, Adolphe! Show whose side you're on!'

*

There were mattresses, of course – with flourbag sheets – not usual, quite a luxury. Do luxuries need be clean? The plinth – there were some aspirants, of course. Artists. A severed head. Head of a goat. A skull, a pumpkin hollowed out. Then something the kids had made, that didn't look like anything.

'That one is best,' says Anouk.

All beautiful, all unadorned, and all connected to the humans' history. None show at first what makes them art, why they were fitted on the plinth: none show the relations of production that for sure had made them possible, that must also be reflected in them. Like the child has no logo showing who its parents were.

'We should go, quick,' says Mack. 'Anything is probable, if we stay. An insurrection, great patriotic war, an international force: we hold the cash, Anouk. We wait.'

'There is no choice,' Anouk says, limping. 'The document – it promises. It isn't cash. We'll have to see where Adolphe flies.'

'Everything was prepared,' says Mack. 'They must have known – it was all easy. Adolphe, the room cleared, the door unhinged, the floor replaced.'

'You said politics was easy, Mack,' says Anouk. 'It's like football – that couldn't be more child's play – yet it fascinates till people think it's hard. Remember, Mack! Fortune's a woman – I'm your luck. And all those other people – their lives we saved, they're no longer being killed...'

'Maybe,' says Mack. 'This fortune: a roll of the dice? Or a privilege that lasts?'

'We're only partly complicit,' says Anouk. 'All right, Mack: they'll die, but we won't have paid for it.'

'Everybody dies,' says Mack. 'That's in the song. It's up to you to say "it may never happen".'

'That's the line about us having sex,' says Anouk. 'No sex on mission, that is in the book.'

'You're not in the squad, Anouk,' says Mack. 'And it's me that has the book. Besides – there's you and Adolphe...'

'So what?' says Anouk. 'He'll be back. For this,' and she swirls a bottle with the wormlike thing...

'We bet on Adolphe taking sides,' says Mack, 'Not wondering where the money goes.'

'The guys who're in it for ideals – your people wouldn't contact them. Those are the warriors who get insulted, blacklisted,' Anouk says. 'Shot, too. The dodgy ones – those get our cash.'

'Adolphe said, "Not country, not form of state: what matters is – the original source of wealth – the soil and the labourer." A jacquerie, perhaps? Nothing in our line: not overthrowing Wolf, not fighting for new lands...' says Mack.

'No,' says Anouk. 'Nothing good will come here, nothing is plentiful except the poor. Forget the land, the labour. Wealth? I'm fortune: patrimony and chance. Those are the source of wealth now. Adolphe can't rely on anything that seems more common sense, more present, or more basic than an inheritance and luck. It's all just me: all the initiative is mine. Economics, Mack – that's the current recipe – not politics.'

'And mine,' says Mack. 'Initiative.'

'No,' Anouk says. 'You were trained to be an idler. A gent. That's what attracts you to a crumbling place like this – you spot the bosses – they're the easy ones to deal with.

Greedy and few. All the rest is silent, desperate – you make up your stories about them. They don't care. They're just arms and legs to you – the belly's what is interesting to you guys...'

*

Everybody sleeps. When it's light, Anouk has gone – taking her shoe, her foot, her document.

'I am to blame,' thinks Mack. 'I'd forgotten. Sophie! Act! I tried. I wasn't wise, I was just cunning.'

*

Wolf – has his contests. War internal, and outside. The province so desired – gets its autonomy, guaranteed. A free zone. It's quite like annexation. No one is happy – who would expect to be? Lots of people run and don't come back. Wolf wins – but in the end, he's wobbly. He didn't get the cash – he's run a tab instead. Adolphe – is leader of an opposition that comes and goes – to jail, on committees ... all of that. The grass – is a success, but not so big as it was thought.

'I'll try to get the paper back from Anouk,' says Vivienne.

She'll always love him, Mack, but she's glad he's not too close... Indeed, he's very far away. He can't stand Vivienne.

*

You're called 'Spider'. Your socks are so greasy, they rot your feet, go cold at night. Without them, your boots are crippling you. You can't shoot at anyone because it would give you and your mates away. If they catch you, they nail you to a door – sometimes they'll leave you there, waiting in nature, in the sun; and sometimes not. All the emotions Spider has are laid out like on a stall. Till it's over, the feeling's quite extreme. They'll find out where he's from and let him know that everyone he's liked or hasn't liked – will suffer from him; in their various ways, be nailed.

Mack is an envoy – doesn't suffer much. He thinks – 'It's all regression now. Everywhere there's guys like Wolf, liars and stupid, waggling their million followers like tails glued to a kite. It's all resolved – I'm not. A journey? Someone new?'

Aversion he can feel: Anouk, the great betrayer. Admiration – Sophie. Distaste – Vivienne; bad conscience – Sylvia. Fulvio – the profit. Mack would like Fulvio, maybe even closer, a touch of passion buried underneath... Paco's an idiot, he thinks. He'd love to make out with Aurora, but does he have the qualities...?

From what he sees, they're all mostly heteros, or try to be. They could all couple up, like in an ark, and trip to somewhere. He doesn't know, of course, that it's not all 'bump along' for him.

The global intellect – two projects started. Clouds and bombs. Clouds – the way chance works, and how to make them drift your way. Let the others burn, the thirst, the flames... Bombs – each needs a lot to make the steady state. Fear of death, even in your bunker – there's a maths that keeps you almost safe, trading on the other guy, his weakness, fear of death. Bluff, with a pistol. Human, very human. The science – maybe it can have you push the planet to a better space where viruses all die, but you'll still have a demijohn of them – best not try to tangle with you, or to risk the glass, so thin and iridescent...

★

'Well, Mack, where's Anouk?' Fulvio asks.

'Oh, in the maquis. In a camp,' says Mack. 'And I loved her so...'

'Let's look for her,' says Aurora. 'And don't talk rubbish, Mack.'

'No, Aurora,' says Mack. 'And there's no money. She had a promise, but nothing you could spend.'

'Let's all go and look for her,' says Paco. 'Let's get drunk first. Have a party. Anyone know some songs?'

'I know lots,' says Aurora. 'All in Portuguese. "*Ela è carioca*", "*Tudo se transformou*".'

'Fuck you, Aurora,' Paco says. 'You kill everything before it starts to kick.'

Paco has a can, a can of his movie. 'It's not true,' Paco apologises. 'We weren't there when it happened.'

'Everything happens very quick in there,' says Fulvio, when it's flowed over them. 'Even the deaths. And the judgements.'

'If you want slow,' says Paco, much annoyed. 'Sit outside and watch the traffic lights. Think "history": – green, amber, red. Only – the east is never red for long. Grass, desert, revolution, that's the colours. Then it starts all over. Not for you, Sylvia,' he adds, pinching her wrist. 'You block. You've turned your motor off.'

'Come on!' says Fulvio, hooting like an owl. 'We're friends, comrades. In that VW van – its nose turns towards the conflicts and to poverty. Wealth, mobilisation too, no doubt. We're hugger-muggered in the back, but the van, it always finds the truth. Don't cry, Sylvia – junk those little pugs – we'll find some afghans or some ridgebacks, that's for sure...'

They're not so drunk they can't pile in the van. They're all quite drunk. Paco leaves his movie, on it runs, and the end, the celluloid, flaps free – "flick flick flick" on the projector. It's not why they're called "flicks".

In the back of the van, it's dark: 'Up and down and up again,' shouts Sylvia – 'The sea, the sea!'

'No!' says Aurora. 'It's the Atlas mountains – they tell us where we are... I had one at school. I can hear cicadas whistling through their teeth... This is a hot land – that smells of kerosene: can it be Spain? Chad?'

'No!' Fulvio shouts back: 'We've gone quite a different way – we're where they turned their mass graves into skiing slopes. The women of the East, all beautiful, so delicate – not serious, dancing through their thirteen years. Buy them a bock! God meant them to be prostitutes for sure – but we can't stop... Here – White Russians, white as mozarellas...'

On, on, the van – first Fulvio drives, then Paco – Fulvio prefers a route more northerly. Paco can't resist his Turkey, a spin of the wheel, down they go – those in the back can't tell... but they smell the apricots, the pomegranates, the spring, the almonds... 'Smell! The goats – maybe it's us!' says Mack.

All are still quite drunk. No one expects good taste from drunks.

'Fulvio,' shouts Mack. 'Anouk! We're looking for her, remember. She had a project, a mission... Can you see out the front?'

'We're nearly there, I think,' says Fulvio. 'Feel the grass beneath the wheels.'

'We're in the trees,' says Paco. 'Cameras are useless here – we have arrived in the new land, guys. The empty land. It's up to us! Fill her up!'

Sylvia climbs the little ladder they provide – up on the van's roof, like a thin Cortes. 'It isn't empty, guys,' she shouts. 'It's full of holes!'

'Anouk?' says Fulvio. 'This is Siberia – she's not here. Nor Sophie either – no one can expect a full house of abandoned loves to wait somewhere and have you stumble over them.'

'Song of the forests,' says Aurora, and she roars, like rutting, or a call to all the small forgotten things that flit behind the birches. 'Aoooo,' she cries. 'No one will understand my words, a cry of pain for past and future both grimy, unregarded...'

The van is beached. Abandoned, out of gas. Beneath their feet, it's probably all gasoline, you'd need a probe, a sound, to shake, rustle, pound those leaves and trunks ethereal – then suck, until you've filled the tank...

That, they're far too tired to do.

'On foot! You barge-haulers,' Paco shouts. 'Trudge on, *davai, davai!* Now, find the water, dig the canal – and haul again! You're phantoms, with a phantom barge – there's nothing heavier, the distances are blue and grey – no port, no rest...'

A hundred metres on, they see – a compound, flags of heavens layered up and down – some stupas, guys cutting up blue aloes, some at prayer, some on sun-loungers drinking rum...

'It must be Chagatai's domain,' says Mack. 'The rich, and the devout... The waiters and the maids – nomads with their beasts all dead, the skeletons just ribs and tails, broken umbrellas on the rainless steppe. The scene is parched and cloudless, those jiggling journeys abstract now, just songs and panoramas without end.'

What did he expect? Here – it's orderly, oasis. Why, there's camels. A fifteen minute ride won't cost, it all goes on the bill, it isn't you who pays, it's friendly plastic – slide him in the slot...

'It goes,' says Chagatai, handing out the blinys. 'I'm not as rich as I would like. I don't do charity, but domination of the world is never far from nighttime thoughts...'

★

And down a knoll comes Mister Ji. 'Dear Mack,' he says, embracing, squeezing out his tear. 'I did you wrong. I've not slept since. Yours was the least of them – the accidents. Associates – they never last. I'm in it all with Chagatai – my little outpost. My man- and womanpower. All chasing the big idea, of course. You, Mack – still in the hunt?'

'I lost Anouk,' says Mack, weeping, hugging Mister Ji. 'Wisdom too – it still escapes me...'

'Oh, how I sympathise,' says Mister Ji, pushing Mack away. 'It's a veritable unicorn.'

'Anouk believed in sacrifice,' says Mack. 'It's what drives it on. The world, that is.'

'It's true, so true,' says Mister Ji. 'Those are the pure, the selfless ones – we common sort, we watch, and hope their sacrifice won't fall on us as well.'

They sit by the pool.

'Bring us the usual, my dear,' says Mister Ji to one of the monks. It's a pitcher of manhattans: 'We're all Robinsons,' says Mister Ji, pouring. 'You and I, at least. We drive the ship on the rocks – oh no! The regret! We sing out our fate ... all those poor souls, sacrificed, and only we survive. That piece of rock to cultivate, make a civilisation, acculturate the savages, have them build a ship, find a crew, just so's we can sail away and tell our tale, inspire the young settlers to follow us. Religion, Mack: we cry out the psalms, the song of Solomon – fantasy, Mack. Sex! I'll bet you've had every one here – the ladies, and the gents, I bet. It's what we do, while we await the moment... the epiphany. I've had that too, of course. You, me, and Chagatai: we're history, life in a cocoa pod, waiting to burst out, make the world fragrant and alert.'

'What's the plan, Ji?' Mack asks, overwhelmed. 'Love and wisdom...?'

'Oh screw those,' shouts Mister Ji, calling for another pitcher. 'You sound like my poor unfortunate associates, the mess they left me in. Chaos, Mack. I'm having to sort it out. Love and wisdom? Try sex and winning instead. For those others – you need two lives at least. Sorting things out – you did that with Wolf and Adolphe. You can't have everything, Mack – and nor did they. Make peace with Vivienne – you'll have more power and cash than you can spend or fit in cages...'

'There's an edge of cynicism, in you, Ji,' says Mack.

'No, Mack,' says Ji. 'I'm the Master. *Your* Master.'

'You laugh, Ji, laugh like the wind sweeping everything away. There is no end to the world... No end to where everything goes...'

'Well, Mack, we just don't know, because it's gone,' says Ji. 'But you're wrong about the end of the world. It has no end because it's round. But – very finite. You're Robinson, you board the ship, you have your sample case... They think you bring bad luck, but they don't know... It's science, bodes no good. You bring no yam, no limes, no breadfruit. you're no fucking use, poor Mack...' and Ji laughs hugely.

'It's true,' says Mack. 'Those guys – their teeth will all fall out. They'll eat the goats, they'll have huge sores, no sleep at night, they'll be sewn in their shrouds – just a funeral party left, the captain sleeping far below... A tender moment – the ship's cat, over she goes – the old salts weep, the first time, their mates – "better you than me," they thought ... but Katerina Kat – no, that's too much. You take the wheel – maybe you had limes concealed... you're healthy, teeth standing to attention ... you know bugger all about the wheel – it turns; the ship, of course, it can't. Down, down you go – the rest's the tale we know. Empire, Mack! A dirty word? It's all we have. Aurora – she's dispensed with words – and she has nothing, Mack, nothing at all! A filmy image on a film! Empire, Mack – it's the best, the biggest, we can do.'

'I don't understand,' says Mack. 'I followed a good person, that is all.'

'Anouk? She's good? You've lost her, Mack,' says Ji. 'We must go on with what we've got – bad and powerful, if we must.'

Mack calls a monk – the monk ignores him. 'Don't do that,' says Ji. 'They're not good, but they're not slaves.'

'What then?' asks Mack. 'Your plan, dear Ji?'

'Fresh pastures, Mack,' says Ji.

'But – the beasts are dead. The guys here ride on motorbikes,' says Mack. 'They're reading for their doctorates so they can leave...'

Ji ignores him. 'What you must do,' he says. 'If you want anything – territory, threat, or revelation – is ignore what lies between you and your goal. Ask Chagatai. You go until you can't. Forget the climate and the rest – pressures from east, weakness in the west – prepare the ground, careful, careful – and then get on your steed... Better still, have some guys carry you where wheels won't turn...'

'This is work in progress, Ji,' says Mack.

'Of course,' he says. 'Some things don't work. I'm not interested in the countries – they're all the same, would like to be – satisfied with being top, or middling, even cute and

tiny. That's no fun. Or you can try to have your legions
hidden everywhere, but signing to you – an exercise, a sport
... religion or a guru...'

'Those are found out,' says Mack, playing along:
'Besides – this mystic stuff, the "live for ever", "live the
better" stuff – not only does it fail, it lands you – well, you
end in jail, or worse.'

'Exactly so,' says Ji. 'I have in mind a subtler thing.
Imagine something quite extreme, and tenuous... Suppose
you have a stick, a cane, maybe of a wood that's only found
in one small place, a forest it's dangerous to enter and to
roam around...'

'I don't need a stick to walk,' says Mack. 'You mean –
trade, Ji. Consuming the same articles, you have a secret,
an affinity... No, Ji: it's vapid. There's no personality, no
profit, and no loss. It's best to be a corporation, invest –
pull strings. Or know the secrets, carry the knowledge of
hidden things – an engine, in a gladstone – that you
manipulate... Better than an idea, or a faith, state project...

'No, Ji,' Mack goes on. 'I've been through this, even with
Anouk, on a small scale, we tried some futures out. No –
the truth becomes banal. I fear the search goes on – indeed,
we've lost Anouk, but we remain the same, the loss fits into
the reality that we all make. It is a loss – but it's reality, a
gain, a profit, even. No, Ji – we're back at wisdom. That
was Sophie's gift, that slips out of its envelope, out of the
box, the parcel, even as she hands it to you, turns away,
forsakes...' and Mack, like Sylvia, is weeping now. 'And
disappears...'

'What a let-down, Mack,' laughs Ji. 'I'm sure you'll find
her – but it's clear, she couldn't bear the time she spent
with you, trying to show you something, who knows
what...'

'You could settle, Ji,' says Mack, exasperated. 'For a chain of these resorts, in barren places, taking these broken histories, and making cash... A Shangri-La convenient, luxurious – "Near you, and you, but probably not you..."'

'I'll think about it, Mack,' says Ji, much disappointed. 'The guys here – they don't invent gadgets and cures. Those are just temporising anyway. They see the monotheistic gods are angry spiteful babies, that having lots of them is opera. But the wisdom that they seek? Nothing, Mack. Trumpets and tea, Mack: tea and trumpets. You have to look elsewhere. Like I do.'

Chagatai interrupts. 'You two – you talk as if your lives are rehab. You have to believe in it all, as you pass through. Those piles of skulls – they're horses' – they got tired. That's why you see the ribs and tails, out on the steppe – the souls are in the heap, the skulls – a kilometre high.'

'That's all gone, Chagatai,' says Ji, angry at the eavesdrop.

'I'm up here,' says Chagatai, gesturing. 'I ride my horse, down there – he's my neighbour. He's in order, he keeps the line. I tell him where to go, if he's worn out – there's others, always have been, always are.'

'You?' Ji laughs. 'You ride China?'

'Oh,' says Chagatai. 'You need to know your history. It never stopped. It's a marriage.'

'You're dreaming, Chagatai,' says Ji.

'That's how it seems,' says Chagatai.

There's peace. This is how it ought to be, for ever.

'Look, Mack,' says Chagatai. 'You are my friend, you funded me. You're here for ever, free. No sweat. But – your friends – in short, they have to pay.'

'Until that Vivienne decides...' Mack starts...

'They'll have the choice,' says Chagatai. 'Be monks or waiters, pool cleaners and the rest. Meditate, eat bad. Or bustle round, and have what's left, and milk the camels too...'

'The van is empty,' says Mack, in despair. 'Can you find some gas?'

'We made a vat,' says Chagatai, 'of manhattans. I'm sure it runs on them.'

'Sylvia is off,' says Ji. 'Into the trees. Looking for samoyeds.'

'Paco would stay – his movie's formulaic, every one's the same. The actors change...' says Mack.

'We can provide,' says Chagatai. 'No doubt he'll want some battle scenes. That enters in my plan,' and he and Ji exchange a glance. 'They could even want a contract here.'

'Paco has given his body to the world,' says Ji. 'Those tattoos go from out to in. He has a shaven head, I think, beneath the blue – on top, there's clouds and cranes – a filigree – he will do fine work as a monk. Sylvia's an outdoor type – she'll make a little paradise, a garden where there's limes for the tequila, cider apples, sugar canes – and pears... There's no snakes in Mongolia!' and they laugh, Ji and Chagatai... '*Le vin du souvenir*,' says Ji.

'There is a flaw,' says Mack. 'With Fulvio. The committee he and Sylvia are on – if they don't show – then special forces might invade...'

'Oh, that's an excellent exercise,' says Chagatai. 'We'd see them off, staple Fulvio to a door, or even boil him – blood must not be shed, you understand.'

'It's all quite different,' says Mack. 'From what I'd hoped. They've reached their end, my friends – but I've found no one. Rather, I've lost. My quest...'

'Don't be so down,' says Chagatai. 'One person will accompany you, your van, your aspirations. Aurora. We don't want her here – she's weird. and moody too. Take her – it's what you always wanted, now it's come true.'

'She doesn't navigate,' says Mack. 'She only eats things you can never find...'

'That's the challenge, then,' says Ji. 'That's what you crave. Maybe she's pregnant – for sure, it's not by you. You'll start a colony, a crew, a caravelle of exploration, settlement where no one's ever been...'

*

'There's shouts and tails,' says Aurora, as they're moving off. 'It's Sylvia! She's found her samoyeds – they've engulfed her: now, they are one.'

'That's terrible,' says Mack, as the van weaves its tapestry through the taiga. 'Still, I left a bookmaker and a bonze – that isn't bad.'

Aurora is a pain. She has the problem with the window and the door. Getting her out and in's a puzzle – till she's trussed and silenced in the back. 'Now, dear Aurora, what's your liking, dear? Shall it be mince? Or quince? A bowl of zhizhi? Eat, and go on practising your hums...'

'Oh how I miss Paco,' Aurora moans. 'There was him. Then there was his body – a fresco of all you'd want to know – the arabesques and swags, first and last words...'

'He's found his set,' says Mack. 'He's looked for that throughout his life. He can do without a camera now...'

'No,' says Aurora. 'He was the wall. What it hid, himself – he'd tell, but you'd not understand. Then, on the wall – his story. A tale of everyone, a Chinese theatre, without brakes, where utmost fantasy's expected – the spectators must take the road, become quite other, join the throng of soldiers, merchants, spirits divine and not, the animals – some hobbled – and the birds, all caged. The birds – they sing. Everybody sings. It is a place of freedom – but not for you, not as you are, for all the things you're not, will never be. That's true freedom, Mack. Not being you, being the picture on the wall.'

'It's still him,' says Mack bemused. 'Paco. Sitting beside you on the bus. Swimming in the pool, a story long as whales, up and down, shallow to deep and back again...'

'No, Mack,' Aurora says. 'You haven't understood. He's solved the puzzle, by himself, in and on himself. Eternal culture or the civilisation, the Volkisch earthy part – the history, the clubs set in with teeth, arrows with bloodied flights... He's overcome the contradiction. He moves among you – everywhere: his skin is unique, but the message, tale – is there before you ... or it disappears, into the brothel or the betting shop – then out again, and so: eternal. Imprinted. If he should die, they'll flay him like a god and give him, rather, give his skin – as a cape, a Weltenmantel...

'It should be me, Mack. I should have his skin.'

'I'll let you off, Aurora, you can go back to the resort, the monastery, wait for him to slough, take it all on, add the incantations, the wordless chant – more evocative than any poetry, not binding to a person or a place, but to the earth itself,' says Mack, starting to grasp... 'To what communicates, but has no speech, no eye that's looking on, no mirror, no lens: no interpreter, no lie, no priest, no scientist... Go back, Aurora, if you must.'

'Forget that, Mack,' says Aurora with decision. 'I'm an artist, not a maid.'

They drive on in silence. There are countries, there are rivers, sometimes it snows.

'Anouk, then,' Mack asks. 'Where is she?

'Oh,' Aurora says, 'she's with the Volk. That's where love resides. Can't keep its hands down by its sides – always seeking handholds, grappling, sucking and – delusion, the postcoital state it thinks is peace. Well – yes! it is. Pax eterna, Mack. Not even flames – it's the sound of life, gurgling out, the pitcher holed, losing everything. A spasm, Mack. Damp sand.'

'I disagree, Aurora. I think it is all one... Without a contradiction...' Mack starts. 'Everything.'

'You cretin!' shouts Aurora. 'Treachery! Humanism! Interclassism! There's no class context for you, no struggle... No bourgeoisie... No stools to fall between. Historicist! Relativist!'

'And you, Aurora,' Mack shouts back. 'You have no message. It's all an automatism. No vanguard – just a state that preys. Essentialist! Dogmatist!'

'Yes,' says Aurora, sulking. 'And I'm proud of it.'

*

'Let me off here,' Aurora says. 'What I wanted – was lamb with apricots. You might have guessed. I'll soon be with Anouk. She's been in the fight. Like Ji and Chagatai – they're planning a great thing... Ponies – they're collecting them.'

'Why?' Mack asks. 'They're in a place that's troubled, but it doesn't need the humans there to start a quarrel. See what happened to the beasts.'

'Let's stick to Anouk then,' Aurora says. 'She's a splendour, she's beyond our help and our concern. But if you ever meet again with Sophie, she will ask, "What happened to Sylvia, Mack? She was troubled, wherever it was she went." You'll say, "It was a terrible, an unprecedented thing, it stays with me, nested on my head – there it will be for ever... Nature got her." Sophie'll say "That's right, Mack – she deserved a better end, you're right." And you'll have lied, Mack. You were indifferent.'

'Why get off here, Aurora?' Mack asks. 'It's rather squalid – there's lots of other places similar, and nearer where we want to go.'

'I know what it looks like, what I want,' says Aurora. 'But not quite where it is.'

'Then you won't find it,' says Mack, losing patience.

'That doesn't matter,' says Aurora. 'You and I, Mack, we want quite different things, I'm sure – neither of us will get a part of them. It's all gone by, we're in glass cases in a museum that's been looted and rebuilt too many times. Your quest and my escape – we're ghosts of dusty lizards, my dear Mack. We care because all we want is dead and gone – we care, we mourn for ever, the others don't. Mischief, Mack – that's the best we can still do, and end like Sylvia, eaten by her dogs.'

'There's the door,' says Mack, pushing her out. 'A window too. Enter and exit – they are much the same.'

'I'll join that line,' Aurora says. 'They're maybe handing out some tents,' and she joins a file of ragged people.

'No!' Mack shouts. 'That line's for camps – or deportations. They'll send you back to Chagatai!'

She doesn't hear. She stands expectantly, perhaps she hums.

★

Aurora – in her white caftan, a plastic rainsheet. Be careful!
You become – not what your fellows in the line might be,
but what the guy says you are who sits and writes it down.
Hungarian? Romanian? Both? It's not at all what she's been
looking for. 'No,' she says, 'neither of them. I'm maybe one
of those...' and she points over to a group that's larking
round.

She's not – but you must be something that you're not.
'Aurora!' Mack shouts out. If she hears, she doesn't turn.
You must know, you always do, if the line you're standing
in is wrong.

Mack thinks, 'I'm a lie, looking for something, looking
for nothing – the gestures, movements, tickets, riding
lessons – are identical. Something, nothing – what interests
me is that something follows after something else. It
wouldn't if they nailed you to a door. If there aren't doors,
nailed to the ground, there's always some of that.

'Vivienne,' he thinks, 'that's the next stop.'

*

Aurora. He never sees her again. They'd never have made a
go of it anyway. He misses her. She gets back in the van.

'I hear Vivienne's packed up,' Aurora says. 'You're not
her friend. She's not giving out the cash today. Forget her.
You imagined each other. And we're not communists,
Mack – that would make things worse for us. It's the
answer no one wanted. Don't you ever learn, Mack? I'm
not your girl, I'll never be that, Mack. The dogs of war,
Mack, everywhere – herding the sheep.'

'I think I'll dump the van,' says Mack. 'Where'll we go,
Aurora? Of course, you've a career...'

'Oh Mack,' Aurora says, 'there's always work abundant –
look at Anouk. Adolphe is a hero or he's dead, far off. She
never sees him, she does humanitarian stuff – she helps the
orphan kids. She hates it, everybody hates it. She wishes
they'd all die – I think that she's a spy and steals their food.
They're too small to kill her, so they threaten her. Escape –
that's what they want, be refugees somewhere: they're kept
in the camp because they'll be needed for the homeland –
Soldiers! ... They're really fun, they don't mean harm,
besides, they can't do much of that. It's all a drag, they're
better off confined than hiding in the woods. No one
wanted this – you'd need be crazy to! – she doesn't and
they don't. It shouldn't be like this. No one wants to pay to
keep these dirty kids – if they survive, they'll cause trouble
all their lives, or kill themselves quite soon... Salt of the
earth, Mack. There's photos of them, looking topical.'

'So, you'd news of Anouk? That whole continent – looks
like it's going *facho*,' Mack says.

'My career?' Aurora asks. 'My stuff is rather static. What
I have to do – is do it in ever-larger spaces. That's how you
spread yourself.'

'Did you ever make money with it? Your act? Career?'
asks Mack.

'It's much much more than that,' she says.

Mack drives on – they're both tired, with staring through
the screen.

'You and I, Mack,' Aurora says. 'We have no plot. We
shan't be burnt for our beliefs. If our legs hold out, we'll
find another game, our last button staked – love, wisdom,
still on the table, the banker's tail hangs unforeseen and
forked behind his chair.'

'Well, Aurora,' Mack says, 'you were right about
forsaking speech. Words. They are obsolete – the poetry

with words, it died. A little matter, that's for sure, but it's diffused to everything. My time in Brazil – quite terrible. How sensible, Aurora: rise up singing in the dusk – no word, no presence, no beginning – and you know the end, no 'it may never happen...' Sing! ...

'Now, Ji is interesting. He's waiting for a piece to break, the centre holds, the rest is undermined – then the big glaciers will thaw, the empty spaces – can you hear the hooves, Aurora? A renegade, you'd say. Or the new age? Those resorts – like corporations, cults, caliphates, they're innocent – so are those wars, invasions to bring truth, justice, the aid that goes to bad guys... Ji and Chagatai – everyone's a Jenghiz, Aurora, however they start out... Then – it reaches – its end, the *limes*, starts to retreat, assimilate – the spies surround it, creep in your ears...'

'They'll know the friends of Ji,' Aurora says. 'They'll spy the friends he's dumped, as well as those who got away. You'll be identified, however far you go.'

'Be reassured,' says Mack. 'The strain is everywhere, things fall to pieces. One or two of us ... we just don't count. Were we in Master Wolf's domain, his sights – we'd have to run... That country's small. Elsewhere, we're wires, each one is plaited thick on to a hank – big as an arm, an oak, a ship... We're quacking ducks that sit...'

*

They dump the van. Perhaps some museum...

Mack says: 'Empire is a crime, Aurora, whichever way you see it. What sort of crime? It isn't clear, and if and how there's punishment, and then – who for? I've been everywhere. I've seen the warlords, Ji, and Chagatai, looking for their space. Ah, the taiga,and the steppe! Riches and ghosts, Aurora! Who can resist? I've seen the strategists – the nimbly fingered Fulvio, and – poor Sylvia – the incautious dead. I've seen the interesting parts, Aurora, the projects everywhere.

'I've reached a conclusion, the conclusion ending it, the everything. The last stretch, the twilight: artificial light, of course. It must be – a sort of communism. I know – it's what no one wants. But it's the only way to reach extinction – that's inevitable – with wisdom. Wise extinction – that's the term I need. The details – I shall work them out. I wouldn't want those exams staged, like they make them sit in China. The clever ones are served – and then, all's torn apart, traduced, a scramble. Mine, Aurora, is a delicate task. Don't cry! Extinction isn't massacre, it's slowly drip and drop away. The last pair – females, prowl on different continents, no one sails, or swims to them... It is recessional. Look at the stars – too far away to help, of course, and each has known the story, identical – creatures of all kinds, the octopods, the lichens – each creeping and writhing to their end, the food chain bursts apart, genetic trees fall down – the same parabola. It happens everywhere, Aurora, always the same way. On, on it goes. The word – what can it be, the word sounding over those blank spaces, the dark holes that squeeze you till you squeak? Beware! Me today, and you tomorrow: mihi hodie – tibi cras! And yet there's some who pray to someone who's supposed be responsible!

'The response – is dignity. Accept, delay – even prevent – as long as possible – the fledglings come and go, the eggs – give forth new life, or end, boiled, in sandwiches. Where's the harm, Aurora? Forward, Aurora, *vperyod*! Dignity, respect... And your song rising above it all...'

'You're elegaic, Mack,' Aurora says, 'but – maybe you confuse me with the lark. I'm off the ground – but not that far! The lark is dawn. I'm dusk, and intimate. Brown: not invisible and blue on blue...'

'You could sleep at dusk,' says Mack, 'like all the others do – except the bird of wisdom, Athena's owl – she's always on the prowl, for things the rest of us don't eat...'

'Come on, Mack!' Aurora says. 'If you're in the biz, your gigs are in the night. Besides – you see the stars? They're embers of a terrible rage. I sing and hope they don't fall on our head. The heat, Mack! It will burn us all – with cancers or the thirst... The stars were flung – that's what the poem says – into the calm of nothing, the void, the matt. What rage? A project botched? Or just an anger – loneliness, frustration – maybe a pot of fire that overturned, where the mannikins, the amphoras, the sickles – they were baked – something went wrong...was wrong from the beginning. The Word, Mack! An almighty FUCK! perhaps ... resounding for ever and for ever... And now, we sing, we roll and rock to keep the fires above from tumbling down on us, and the fires within from their explosion... There is no remedy, dear Mack. On with the show, they say...

'A sort of communism,' she repeats. 'Details – over a lifetime, to be worked out, if anyone is listening.'

She thinks, they think... she says, 'I'm not sure I want to hang around for that. I fancy something quicker. Snappers, rolls of cash, and flattery ... starting something, Mack. I know someone else will end it – but not me!'

'How does it seem, Aurora? My idea?' Mack asks.

'You'll grow old quick with it,' she says.

★

'Sophie!' shouts Mack, trotting along beside.

'I must run,' she says. 'I'm on TV. Must buy new boots and fragrances...'

'I've understood your counsel, Sophie, now – you're to give it to the world?'

'No,' she says, 'it's a game – I may need to sing.'

'Sophie,' says Mack. 'That's too neat! Banal! Consider – there's more wars – and more people, fewer soldiers, die...'

'Nothing to do with me,' she says. 'I never held an opinion – being wise is not a humanism, Mack. Soldiers now cost too much to have them dent – the precious suits of armour! It's tough, keeping warriors in line, on message! People are more fluid, though, wear cheap clothes. They're more passionate, and their lives are free.'

'I've known warlords, Sophie, been on a committee, seen the guys hung up...' says Mack. 'Your unconcern ... it puts me on the spot...'

'Aha!' she says, thrusting him back as she finds the store... 'That's a snooker term, I think. Play lots of it, and pool. Takes your mind off battle, and the balls ... make you think of planets, so far off, we'll maybe wave... A hundred years, and we'll exchange a signal – if those guys have eyes, of course – and share experiences of being in the universe. Our poetry, our tales, dear Mack – that's what they'll want to hear. We'll pass like pirate ships, both searching for the gold, the slaves, the empty lands scented with clove and nutmeg...'

'We could be in dodgems, too,' says Mack, deeply disappointed.

'Yes, indeed,' she says. 'I see you've learned the lessons well. Those aren't so difficult, if there's no headstrong scholar round, touting some perverse slant.'

'I've been everywhere, seen them all – bounced off the people – muddled a country. Now, what's left?' asks Mack.

'Fun, Mack,' says Sophie, trotting off. 'After the bird of wisdom does its dreary flight – it's night! Lights, Mack! Music! No one can see what you've been up to, in those dark laurel coppices... You could plait a wreath! Not mourning, Mack – think victory!'

*

Here's a chandler's: quite rare in this town, on the desert's edge: 'SOIT' says the hoarding, 'que l'Abime blanchi étale furieux DU FOND D'UN NAUFRAGE'.

'Supplies for shipwreck and survival our speciality. Waterproof Bibles and Qur'ans ... slave collars, hard tack and oakum... Sealed bottles, messages in Esperanto...'

It's heavy stuff – who can carry that great load?

6

MIRKO

'FULVIO SAYS to look you up,' says Mirko, sidling
by. 'I am his goodson – the son he'd like to have:
obedient and deferential, modest and bright. You
thought that Fulvio lived by beating chance. He
doesn't live like that – he drew me from the pack. No,
Mack – it isn't chance, it's maths. If you're a gambler – the
worst will likely come. Pessimists – like you, dear Mack –
don't party well. At the end, they're left alone, they have to
pay the whitecoats with the big syringe, and as they croak,
the booze is passed around, the medics' fun begins! Not
yours... Avoid it, Mack!'

'My cash,' says Mack, 'it set them up, Ji, Chagatai – and
cast poor Fulvio down. I feel no guilt – maybe I should...'

'Oh no!' says Mirko. 'He's in line to be head bonze. Back
ambition and above all chance, and hope you'll win, be
right, in systems petrified... You get promoted till your
bubble flies and breaks ... Ji, Chagatai – they have a plan –
they need goodfather Fulvio to work the odds. That part –
it's always fluid. There's the river flux – goes from spate to
dry; the beasts that roam, the proto-indians in the trees ...
then, there's the soil... There's forests there,' he says. 'Not
yet decayed – the trees, the crawly things, the monsters like
sea cows that graze among the coconuts ... of course, it's
hot ... a sauna all the year, the guests strip off and down
they go, under. That's where: under. The living past –

177

that's where it is. You keep their plastic cards... It's an adventure, Mack, like you have never had. You see the dinosaurs, all as it was before the other great catastrophe – that land is theirs, their realm. The naked guests – they run and run, they maybe make a deal. It's paradise. You mightn't think so – but it's what we should have been, if only we'd kept fins and tail, been born from Easter eggs, tossed, scattered, hidden in the groves of pineapple...'

'Just one point,' says Mack. 'To get the odds on anything – it takes the cash. It isn't chance, it's math. The guy who makes the book – he doesn't guess: that's what the punters do.'

'I know,' says Mirko. 'The beauty is – whatever happens, if you are a monk, you get immunity. Fulvio is safe. He holds the cash. Where next? Conquest with a contract? With the knout? Trusting to luck? Russia? China? All the empty lands? Republic of Siberia? You just need the guys, the strings of ponies, all that stuff – illiterates, who ride or drive a truck...'

'Why me?' asks Mack. 'I don't know anyone, or anything. What's behind that iron door – I have a feeling it's eternal, not desirable at all.'

'Fulvio knows!' Mirko says. 'You know your fearsome ladies, the supreme sisters – true, they don't knit now. But – Anouk, Aurora, and Sophie – you're a confidant of each. And as for Fulvio, my goodfather – he says, if you're just cheese, the rats will get you. His answer is – you've to be big cheese. That way, it won't go down their gorge, the gouda, cheddar – they will suffocate. Who would have thought – a Mongol, emperor of China, his forces, family, on the thrones of every place that's civilised. Why? How? Does it end, or just proceed? Those places now – they're

wrecked and bombed. No one sits in peace on anything...
Only the steppe is safe, Mack ... but it's dull – arid too.'

'I still don't understand,' says Mack. 'Why they might
think of all the sweat of conquest – election, infiltration,
speculation, all that stuff – when travel in the mind is cheap
and easy, quite secure. The monks – they have it right.
Don't risk, hallucinate, and trip. Smoke and trumpets –
that's their limousine. No arrow from unclouded skies, no
scimitar, no sudden death... No death at all...'

'I can't tell you the whole tale,' says Mirko. 'You don't
just wreck – you build the hostels, the hotels, banks, the
parks for diggers, graders, dozers – the whole shoot.'

'My women!' Mack says. 'Two are having fun, and one –
Anouk – is trapped... There's been a death. It's all been put
down on celluloid – whatever they use now – the whole
shoot, Mirko.'

'Fulvio remembers friends. Families – great
disappointment. Forget the rest, remember him, my dear
goodfather. Friends – those are the best,' says Mirko,
slipping his dry hand in Mack's. 'It's a saga. Paco shoots it
all – he is a dead-eye.'

'It's true, Mirko,' Mack says. 'Those ladies – didn't bring
me love. Nor peace, nor twilight songs. Instead, there's
fighting all around: – here, there are arsenals and soldiers –
so many men and bombs, mobilise, prime, drop – the globe
would fracture in an hour. You might be right – if from the
East arrive the men with dogs' heads, ears like blankets –
who'd be surprised? Who'd be shocked? It's all – another
tale.'

'I don't think there will be wonders,' Mirko says. 'Things
you don't suspect, or violence greater than what you have
already seen,' and he laughs. 'Keep cool, Mack – you have
seen the ultimate, the path to get here, where we are...'

'Yes, Mirko. But I don't want to be a bonze,' says Mack. 'True, I watch. But – I don't believe: I'm not a martyr. I don't pray for anything.'

'That's the best deal,' Mirko agrees. 'Now, I'll move my stuff, my lady, in with you, and have the history begin anew...'

'We'll have to look around,' says Mack, reluctantly. 'For Fulvio, for friendship, I suppose... A room, some mattresses...'

'Oh Mack,' laughs Mirko. 'This way – think! Revelation! With us three lodging hugger-mugger, what you call "a sort of communism" begins.'

'Where are you from, goodson Mirko? What do you eat?' asks Mack, much irritated.

'Oh Mack,' says Mirko, delighted to have needled him. 'I'm from an egg. Imagine, on the earth that rolls around, a heavy egg, quite still and grave. Gravity's its friend. It feels the rocks, the soil, go rushing past, and every bird and rat and hungry human too – you get to know them all, and everywhere.'

'Your goodfather – he had that kind of idea – heavy, and rolling,' Mack says, now quite entranced.

'Oh,' Mirko says, with a disarming grin. 'I don't go for that Mongol-Islam stuff. The Mongols started off as animists: that's how they're known. Rather an insult – it is what I am... It's scientific too – everything, that's lived or not, it has its charge, its energy, its bounce... I don't know why they pray to that, or even sacrifice – you're full of just that stuff itself, so what you make obeisance to, pretend to communion with – is really you yourself, your thrust, idea, your aspiration. If you see my girl – you'll understand. She's like white rubber – if you see us, twined together, quite a colour contrast, as you'll see. You'll be impressed –

she's the unboniest creature in the world. Nothing, no stick, no knob, no boss – nothing, no contact to make you squeal. She's jointless... you could try to take her off me, Mack. There's no skeleton beneath that might resist. It would be natural, you with your cocky walk, the way you keep your prick at ease within your pants... It keeps me on *qui vive*, you bet.

'You see, Mack, there's ideas behind most people: the Yanks, Chinese, Jihadis: being right, being at the centre, being the centre of all things. Do you think ideas have energy? Or is it that they're energy itself, like what births the stars, makes them collide and die in sparks and crumbly crusts? The energy goes on, of course, but you don't see it, where it goes, vanishing up itself...'

Mirko laughs, expecting Mack, perhaps, to object, to laugh with him... something else? Some reaction?

'Where's your girl?' Mack asks. 'You're quite a sexist – probably inherited from Fulvio. Are you what they call a couple? Do you carry stuff, possessions, all that? Clothes, things you stash away.'

'It's held up somewhere,' Mirko says. 'Where there's fighting, there's nothing you can do. Household removals – there's energy, I guess, but no priority, and no idea. Take a chair: it isn't Han, you can't say it's *takfir*, nor Unamerican – it hasn't taken sides; it doesn't have distinction, Mack.'

'I know,' says Mack. 'But if we find a place for all of us – what – as a goodson – do you plan to do?'

'Oh Mack,' says Mirko, 'I do what I'm told, and then I guide you where your will implies you want to be.'

'I know your sort,' says Mack, half joking. 'You want to boost me up, fame or thereabouts, then rob me of it...'

★

Lily – yes, unclothed, as you imagine her, as soon as she's in view – she does recall white rubber – though she doesn't flop, bend out of shape, nor goes rigid like a tractor tyre ... she's just a human woman, as the classifying goes, white rubber, setting off Mirko's non-white, or maybe anyone's non-white idea ... though naturally, this is all a fantasy ... she has no hand in being quite remarkable, or in other ways quite dull.

'I'm not staring at you, Lily,' Mack says. 'I'm imagining your furniture. You managing to sit, upright...'

'Don't rush,' says Lily, holding Mack and Mirko by the hand. 'You may gnash your teeth – I am serene. My loving wisdom – wait! – and a portion might be yours. Or – there could be strife. You see, there's no gooddaughters – love or hate, but not obedience: no gophering for me!'

'And, Lily,' Mack asks, entranced, 'could it be – you sing, some strophes as the sun goes down?'

'You naughty boy,' she laughs. 'Forget what it is you want, and think of me,' and she squeezes Mack's hand with fingers filleted.

'We travellers, Mack,' says Mirko, relaxing on a bench. 'Like us two – we're all Italians. We have to be: Jesus. Illiterate. Full of Southern blarney, and for that the Romans tacked him up – they'd do it now, the bastards, and with rusty nails. Every picture of him done in Italy, of course, and all his family picturised... Mah Po Lo – another illiterate. The Persians told him how it was out east – that stuff about the mandarins, peeing down straws – that's what our mind picks on, dear Mack. The detail sticks: piss and blood – that's what our lives are made of, you and I. What are you, I wonder ... what made you? Scampia? Secondigliano?'

'Where's Lily from?' asks Mack.

'Oh, borne in on a shell,' says Mirko. 'A lovely *cozza!*' and they laugh, Mack maybe against his nurture. Lily pinches Mirko, her thumb and finger like a paper bookmark, signalling a page... 'Mirko can read!' she tells Mack. 'The *Secret History of the Mongols* and of everybody else. He is a master. He'd write them all, if they were unwritten. Now – it's your turn, Mack, your secret history...?'

'It's to come, I fear,' says Mack, shaking with the apprehension.

'They mostly are,' says Mirko. 'But then they're very short.' They laugh, Lily and Mirko. 'The Gospels,' Mirko says. 'What a confusion! Po Lo – there's no original! Don't trust what you haven't read, Mack, and what you have – still less! I'm the goodson, though, remember! I shall write your truth. No fear!'

'When your chairs arrive, Mirko,' Mack says. 'You and Lily'll have to sleep on them. I'm not Fulvio's goodson. What's your orders? What does he expect of me?'

'You can have more than one goodson, Mack,' says Mirko. 'A sort of communism, that's your mantra. There's no party, there's no orders. You've had your party, Mack. Everyone's mucking in together now. The common man, the common woman – we're in the Winter Palace, and we give the orders; exactly what we want, we do. Blow it up, have a feast, make some pics – have a blow up, have a blow out.'

'Come on, Mirko,' Mack says. 'It can't be money Fulvio wants. My source is dry. Contacts? They've gone, Mirko, they took my dawn and dusk. My love too, and the dance.'

'I told you, Mack. Friends,' says Mirko. 'You can believe that, surely? One thing hooking on to other things – the continuity, making you feel good. The species being.

Everybody going everywhere, not bothering with invites and ambassadors.'

'Passing it on, feeding it back,' says Mack. 'That's not me, not at all. Spy. A conduit.'

'A pivot,' Mirko says. 'The point that joins two worlds. The two halves of the universe, the yin, the yang, what you see and now you don't. The history, the future – it's all you.'

'I'm not happy with myself, it's true,' says Mack. 'Left alone, there's not much you can do. Here's the chisel in your hand – and there, amid the rocks – your rock. A marble, big as Athena's house, and hard as hell. What have you got? Athena's bird that flits around and craps upon your sculptor's hand...'

'Wear gloves, then,' says Mirko. 'If you're a namby, Mack. Remember – it is all a front: Chagatai has a hotel in arid lands, his guests are varicose. Mongols are few – they laugh, they sing, their future's shaky and their past ... is best forgot. Islam is fratricide. So – where's the plot? An ear, big as a blanket, listening in to all the chat – that's what you need, Mack...'

'I don't believe there's anything,' says Mack. 'Ji and Chagatai talk big. Fulvio is bored with life – the merrygoround – you leap upon a horse, it turns into a cock, a car, a unicorn. Then, maybe, you get another turn. It's dull, dear Mirko. It's for frustrated guys who can't do good or bad...'

'That's so,' says Mirko. 'Fulvio's in intelligence: he turns each leaf, each grain of corn – what's written underneath. Slices each eggplant – what message is within...?'

'I'm quite dried out,' says Mack. 'I don't care about the future and its secrecy. It's always hidden – yet it comes, each detail laid with brushes of a single hair. I'm dry now, Mirko, parched. I'm white bone...'

'Don't put your bone in Lily, then,' Mirko kids and laughs. 'You're a good guy, Mack, and you'll do what you are told. You want to be a goodson – just you've never found the right goodfather, that is all.'

★

'I have nothing,' Lily tells Mack. 'That means I'm the prize.'

'I want none of this,' says Mack. 'I'm not Mirko's dog. And with communism – we are equal, Lily. We don't fool around. No tricks.'

'If you're his dog,' says Lily, 'you must have a bone. Mirko says. "Don't put that bone in Lily."'

'No,' says Mack. 'I am the bone. It's all of me, it's what I want. On the sand, in the sun, appetite burned up.'

'It's very intricate,' says Lily, hugging Mack. 'You may need to make the sacrifice – if you're his dog, I'll get your bone, maybe you as well... Not what I want. I don't want a skeleton inside. Laugh at my body, pigs, if you must: I am the best! I just don't want those spokes and struts left lying round, some other dog running off with me...'

'Mirko shouldn't bargain with us in this way,' says Mack, much drawn to Lily. 'Although, it's all a bargaining. Good and bad – you get your say, it's all in codes: there's excuses; time and place show you the exits, the escapes, the getting off – like in a crashing plane. They only show and tell you at the last. Usually – there's no one there at all, and down you go. It's all the same.'

'It isn't me,' says Lily. 'Not this tone...'

'Believe me, Lily, it isn't me. It comes from Mirko ... degrading you, degrading me,' Mack says.

'Oh, it isn't him,' says Lily. 'Though you are all the same. It's all a plan, of sorts.'

'If it isn't Mirko, then it must be Fulvio,' says Mack. 'Unless it's all a fiction, made up, an ending quite the opposite of what we'd thought. Paco – had you figured – he knows all the plots... There's two – the end, and the beginning.'

*

'Move, move,' shouts Mirko. 'Walk! Forget the chairs!'

The three of them walk along the street. Lily holds Mack's arm. He says, 'My mother – or maybe it was at school, they said to live a logical life. Is this it, Lily? Is it possible? I knew what they meant then – now, it's hard.'

'You realise, Mack,' she says, 'living as a spy – or better, living as Mirko tells you to, it's not an easy way to pass your time. Betrayal? Of what? It's really loyalty, simultaneous, to different sides. You can't take the weight of thinking it's deceit and treachery. No, Mack, it's being fluid. Being jealous too. You know – I'm not a freak. All women are like me – maybe I'm more like them all than others are. Your women, Mack, your destinies – you turned them into people quite indifferent to you, often intolerant – you're rather querulous, you know. It's your fault – you're not adapted to people, especially not to women. They don't change, they're not flighty – that's your sexism, Mack. They don't go after fun – they play along, that's all.'

'Not so fast, Mirko,' Mack shouts out: 'Lily, give me a hand, keeping up.'

'You understand what you must do,' says Mirko, pressing on. 'You ask your side what they propose – what future. Then you tell the other side, and in return, they tell you...'

'It sounds simplistic,' Mack says, out of breath.

'I hope it is,' says Mirko. 'Usually, it gets quite complicated. All you need to do, is tell the truth. You can't go wrong.'

'And that's what Fulvio wants, I guess,' says Mack. 'The truth about it all.'

'I'm sure if he was the pope,' says Lily, hugging him again, 'you'd do it for him. The caliph, presidents – and people with responsibilities too.'

'Spirits,' says Mack. 'That's what they have. There's no harm in telling them, all that they'd like to know.'

'The new things,' Mirko says. 'Not the old quarrels. Diverting rivers, joining them up... The Ob – what use is that? We need the water – now, the animals have gone, or we can finish them ... the Amur...'

'Oh no!' shouts Mack. 'It's sacred!'

'It's dry. It's like the rivers down in Africa – finished, or chemical. New frontiers,' Mirko goes on. 'Mountains raised to divert the clouds, rains upon your lands. The seas paved with silken sheets – so you can walk, holes, for you to aim at fish. Glass bubbles, strings – down you go in them, into the dark. Lily is one of those, the fishy fishers, she loves the pressure, without a backbone, you are one of them – it's black, but there's a bosch, a broth of shapes, all colours, like tree decorations, rainbow baubles, transparent – you see the brain, the heart – shine the light, you see what they – what no one – has ever seen – the blue, the orange...' He shouts, 'Lily! Are you transparent? Can we see your brain, those eyes like dinner plates – seeing nothing? Hear the alarm! Blanket ears! Flee! Eat!'

'People look like what they hunt,' says Lily, much annoyed. 'There's pigs, Mirko. Potatoes too.'

'No offence,' says Mirko, laughing. 'It's all strategic. Competition. They go at each other, 'neath the waves, down among the bones, jousting with harpoons.'

'Worm farms,' says Lily. 'The new grass. The hybrid vegetable: – like the Semurgh did for birds – the vegetable that's like a hundred others, all subsumed. There's your mystery, your sacredness, dear Mack.'

'It sounds banal,' says Mack, 'and drastic, too.'

'Have no doubt, Mack, it's serious,' says Lily. 'It's about the stuff you need to have. Or take.'

She whispers to him, 'Mack – I know you'll listen to me: I'll have a revolution made for you, bigger, better, than you can imagine. Will it last, be worth it – it's up to you. You might back off, of course...'

To Mirko, she says, 'I'm the new, Mirko – that old stuff, love, wisdom, song – those are what you aim for when you're in the dirt and dark. When you toil and starve – those are your wispy angels. All gone! Of course, the new stuff – my new shape, the new shape of everything, the living in an anxious state, counting our beans, drying the mushrooms, waiting for messages – will it last out the heat, the snow, the winds? We're fighting over it already. Earth, water, sand – our precious store. The only thing abundant that we have – is fire. What do you expect? There's not much other left. Of course – there's everything there ever was ... the charge, the prickly charge original – but it's gone from us, rushing away, into the void, away, away it flies...'

'Don't fret,' says Mirko. 'There's always messages that fill the void. They'll tell us when our time is up.'

He pulls them to a doorway. There are steps. 'Down there,' he says. 'You use your ears – there, you can listen in. Then, you must take the elevator – up and up – at the top, it's silent. Maybe you hear choirs a-humming in your ears... That is the wind – it blows, because we roll along one way, the wind blows in t'other sense – faster we go, faster it blows away ... the bad dreams. Time wasted, Mack, the time we spend in mine or office, with our hand or brain, working for capital, for a wage, or for people quite indifferent. There must be a way to cancel all that out, to start again, take different paths. Up on the tower, there's no listening. You see, you watch. And so, you spy on everything, the flatness and the ridge, the last scuts going into lairs...'

'All that, I tell Fulvio?' asks Mack. 'He mills it round, out comes his strategy...?'

'Not strategy,' says Mirko. 'Odds. Just odds – the sods look to themselves,' he jokes. Lily and Mack don't laugh. 'It's what you – we – have always wanted. Knowing everything. Passing it on. Nothing is required of you, but that. You are the pipe – made from your tibia; or the great drain that's sucked and dried the desert. You are the voice, Mack, the melody...'

'This tower,' says Mack. 'These deeps: someone will have placed them there, someone...'

'Forget it, Mack,' says Mirko. 'Do you think the agencies, the states, the guys in macs – haha! – do you think they ask themselves. 'Well! Here is everything. someone must be responsible, and made it all, and made the speed that drives it all away, so fast we'll never see what we have never seen... We know how large is the unknowable, we sell the tickets that might take us where we'll never go, beyond the stars, beyond the limits, the *limes*, if you like, of what was yesterday's ineffable, tomorrow where we'll be ourselves, rushing out, yet with the false sensation that we're sitting still – Lily in her chair, you prowling round. Illusion, Mack! Perspective's lost, Mack, when you're forever borne off to a place you've never been and never seen. Never wanted, never heard of. We're on the move! Rushing to our new space, our empty future. And in our pack, on our back – what's there? – just a hank of grass, some creature's jerked flesh, some pomegranate seeds...'

'That is the task, Mack,' Lily says.

'What?' asks Mack.

'Knowing it all,' she says. 'Keeping calm, and not attaching. Remember Sylvia – passion, vengeance, the tattered divan and the bony thighs: nature got her, swallowed her right up.'

'That was all another life,' says Mack. 'Paco's old movies, guys strung up in birdcage promenade, the morning and the evening songs, the ragas that went on for weeks.'

'New bearings, Mack,' says Lily. 'Take them now and keep on taking them. We're on the move, like Mirko says: the bearings always modify – but we are with you, we are your lode stars. Just – don't look in the sky, we're here beside you,' and she hugs him tight.

*

'Do your best, Mack,' Mirko says: 'And one day – you might be my own goodson.'

'I think of Anouk. She does her best – those kids, seething in that camp. She's good, she does her best...' says Mack.

'Don't try to judge,' says Mirko. 'People tell their tales, how good they are, how justified. Your judgment on them all – quite irrelevant. You're just the nozzle oiling them along. Let's agree – Anouk is good, the best. Her love's a nozzle, oiling kids along. Have done with it! And concentrate!'

'Of course,' says Lily, comforting. 'The void interests me, like everyone. It's where we're headed for – not in a morbid sense, of course, but trailing our ink scrolls, like squids ... being exactly as we are, full of everything as plums... Who'd not be interested in it – the nothing that awaits, so full? Does it sound crass, Mack? Kitsch? Don't let it – I'm disinterested, naturally, but in disinterest, there's always interests. Anouk would recognise – pure love! That's a thing that disappoints when you try it out, but – wow! – it's really something, as a goal! Sacrifice – that is the prize! Disinterest, becoming interest! You, Mack – spy and report. You'll get no recognition, should never be found out. That would spoil it all. Wait. Is being a goodson reward enough? Why – you could be mine! Forget Mirko. My goodson, Mack. Now, there's a thought!'

*

The three live very close, they're more intimate than Mack has been with anyone – their work requires it. For Mack, all day with Lily, Mirko too – is like you have bad children. You love them, of course, but you have to pretend you love them, too. They take him further from the destination.

Of course.

*

No one goes now to Chagatai's resort – Mack thinks of it as Shangri-La, but can't remember what that story is, how it ends, probably no one recalls it any more. Now, the plain is dry, austere, always the featureless. The monks, who don't know anything, eyes closed they chant and hum, maybe don't see it's reedy, cadmium yellows, all dried up around, no memory of water... It's like a medieval castle. Knights and priests. No one comes. No foe, no friend. The tatars – probably they're already there, inside.

Ji is hard; a hard vindictive guy.

All Mack's news goes straight back to Fulvio, plans for survival, plans for war – Fulvio doesn't answer back, there is no need. What can Paco do? Being a waiter – waits? It doesn't matter, you can make a movie out of anything. Love, a musical, an epic, locals pretending to be Japanese, armies and gangs, tarts and madonnas, exploring some psychological theme – mourning, loss of faith, forgetting nature and regretting it, regretting being young, forgetting it: – nothing of consequence.

Mack records it all, and Lily hugs and hugs. Plans and plots, the names of magnates and of torturers – you hear it on the wire, your hear intentions down below, then with your racing glasses – see them jumping into trucks and forming fours and fives, with bags of swank. You tap in, like a blind man, you hack, like a butcher. How the future's planned...

Knowing everything, thinks Mack, doesn't assist that 'sort of communism' – 'No,' says Lily, 'everyone knew everything before you, Mack: it's school, just a rite of passage. Knowledge is a disappointment, just like birth and death. It's all potential, never exactly what you want – it's blossom, not the fruit. Come here,' she says. 'You cheeky boy,' and squeezes him, her long arms fold him in.

7

THE DAM

ANOUK – full of love for people quite indifferent. The sign. There it is – drawn in the sky, 'You can't lose, first bet is free.'

'Salvation – limited: but sacrifice – that's total,' Mack says.

'Go if you must,' says Mirko. 'Remember, though, you're in line to be a goodson...'

'Don't get caught,' says Lily, and she cries. 'You know all there is to know – if they could spoon it out of you...'

'Yes!' Mirko says. 'They'd empty you, and you'd be worthless...'

'But, Mirko – all I know goes straight to Fulvio,' says Mack. 'His is the long spoon...'

'Well,' Mirko says, 'so be it. Come back quick.'

The country's flat. The mountains, conquered, stand above the plain, a dam holds it all back – the water and the rocks. The province sequestered for the good of each. The dam – you need some turbines, wires, and join them up. After the speech, there's light. Spin those wheels, don't touch what's live...

'Lost Boys', says the sign on Anouk's camp.

'I'm lucky,' Anouk says. 'Now. The guys I serve are lucky – in a different way. We don't move, we're not flood water that must be dried, or swept away. Maybe they'll let the dogs on everyone inside; maybe it's the guards who'll be unleashed.'

'Luck?' Mack asks. 'It should have been some other thing. Now, when the wheel stops or starts – the luck is changed.'

'Yes, yes,' says Anouk, drawing back. 'The turbine sticks, it's dark, or else it turns, there's light...'

'Are you in danger, then, Anouk?' asks Mack.

'I'm in a different game,' she says. 'I'm foreign. What happens to me is different from what happens to the boys, the people. Everything and everyone depends on someone else's fancy, what they hope – useful, true, or something else. This place is tiny, Mack: that's meaningless, I know, but it started larger, now it's been ground up, like paprika.'

'And is there books?' asks Mack. 'Wolf, Adolphe – have they written it all down – is there something I could read?'

'Oh yes,' she says. 'In more settled states, the bosses wait till they're pushed out before they write. Here, we are stuck till death, and so you write to set a course. Reading's compulsory, if you can. Here, the last place in the world, the coloured book curls like a scorpion... If you didn't know, Mack, on the world, there's night and day – the same place goes from dark to light. We elect our murderers, Mack, but the night comes every day, the same. For some, as it rolls on, it's light, for others, dark: the dark ones run, the light ones run – to keep in the dark, the light. Night, day – they come just the same. Everybody runs: that's not the answer.'

'I don't run,' says Mack. 'I want a place that's always light, no sweat.'

'I told you, Mack,' she says. 'We're lucky here – we don't know what will happen – that's the best. If we could, we'd run away. If we could, we'd make do, stay.'

'Adolphe,' says Mack. 'Your cruel lover. Do you feel love for that, the cruelty?'

'You love yourself,' Anouk says. 'That's what's left, precious.'

'You'll stay here?' Mack asks. 'You don't seem to make much sense.'

'There's one world, Mack,' she says. 'Whatever you think you've found, this is all one, here, like everywhere else. One world, Mack, no other. No medal with two sides, no mirror where you're beautiful. Here, the guys – it's clans and factions, families. Of course, they have no clans, no families, no factions. They'd stay: they'd run to some other place, anywhere. I told you, it's all the same. You don't forget where you were born. Being born – it stays with you, all your life. Like us all, they have everything. They have nothing. They'd stay, comply, resist, go, find jobs in electricity.'

'The grass,' Mack says, 'the orange dust, the wide streets, wide as fields without a plant... My skull is like a cave, that scene is painted on – something you can't reach to scrub it off. I guess you've never talked to Adolphe... He was broken bad.'

Anouk ignores him, she says,

'You don't understand unless you see – this place runs your place. You're not good, and you don't bring the good. You won't bomb us, but if you do, it's you that suffers first and after, and the after – it's so long. After never ends, Mack.'

'That I do understand,' says Mack, annoyed.

'They love me, my guys – I protect them. They hate me – they say there's never been enough to eat. There's mountains of it, big boxes, empty flour sacks. If you come again, bring little stuff, Mack,' says Anouk. 'Carved things, things you find in fields and desk drawers.'

'Of course,' says Mack.

They stare at each other. 'I'm sorry,' Mack says. 'I find it hard to fit you back in, to anything. Suppose the dam breaks...'

'Well,' says Anouk, 'it's just rocks and water. Lots of mud, rocks in the road. It mayn't reach to you. I guess they would rebuild – you never hear so much about that part.'

8

LILY

'YOU'RE A SAVANT, Mack, in every way,' says Lily, greeting him with a kiss on the forehead. 'You know everyone is different. You're illuminated! Anouk has a situation: herself, and all those people, the bosses too ... it's hard to make your way above all that.'

'They're different, of course,' says Mack. 'People are, you don't forget. Each one. They're coded in that way. It's the experiences, not to mention luck: it's jail, camp ... starvation. They turn out much the same for everyone. People converge, they want the same things. I – they – lose illusions, though: the loss is not just mine...'

'You're wrong about the birds,' says Lily, pulling fast away. 'They chivvy smaller ones, they leave, but they come back from somewhere. The small ones – they don't sing for you, they look for space, a silence they can fill, where they are themselves, a bit of sex, making their circle. Now, tell me, Mack – how was the grass where Anouk is? Is it for eating yet? Will the dam hold back the flood?'

'They say the water'd reach to us,' says Mack. 'It could fill up our deeps, erode the tower. It's just a guess, of course ... there's people too, the water's just behind – they see our high ground, scramble up, they're hard to stop. We'd do the same, it's just our luck, and getting first to places in those odd ships long ago...'

'We're safe,' says Lily. 'On our side we have the maths. The great thing is to calculate your luck, be sure your bets do not impoverish if horses fall and jockeys cheat... The arithmetic, dear Mack. That's what you need, and poorer guys don't have.'

'Of course,' says Mack. 'And being good is often what you want when you begin. Anouk wanted that at first: but good and bad – they're minor things, concerns you change according to other things ... other people, stuff you hear. They're not the news, the good, the bad. What happens in the major keys is quite indifferent to them, and more significant. Heads and brains – from on high, they look like snail shells – hard to see if they are full or been consumed... The blackbird has two ways to judge. Empty or comestible, worth the visit; or to be ignored.'

'Your work, Mack,' says Mirko. 'Is the tops. Spying, seeing where the wind blows to, where it's from. Saving things – the world, your skin. The moral law – where does that come in? The moment when you fall asleep, perhaps. The bird of wisdom ... then, next day... It's gone!'

'Well,' Mack says, 'are you sure I matter?'

'Of course you do,' says Lily, hugging him. 'You're my sweet bundle.'

'They'll reinforce the dam,' says Mirko. 'Send cash to Wolf, and he'll pass some on to those lost boys. Anouk could goad them on, to start a conflict, but they're vulnerable – and, where would it end? Best give them welfare... Keep Wolf sweet.'

'Ah yes,' says Mack, 'Wolf's welfare... It's not a sort of communism, that's for sure...'

'Social democracy, that's what you really want,' says Mirko. 'But people won't. That path – it doesn't lead, it peters out. Forced to be free – remember that! That's the process, Mack. You didn't talk for long with Wolf ... you didn't open Adolphe's cage, or take the risk.'

'Be clean,' says Lily, 'tidy too. I'll be your girl – until you are a goodson, Mack. Then – it could be incest.'

'No one is in the heights for ever,' Mirko says. 'You, like the rest – weren't worthy. So – it's long life – or nasty early death. I can guess which you would choose. You are not worthy, Mack. Neither end's quite suited: is there another way? Senile or premature – they say those are lives, although they're deaths. You haven't lived the life approximate, in the little life you've known. You've been convinced there's something more – one that you can't grasp, and can't attain. Maybe you're the pig dissatisfied, poor Mack.'

'It's true,' says Mack, quite tearful now.

'A holiday!' says Lily. 'Relax, Mack. Go where fancy takes.'

9

'HOTEL CHAGATAI'

THERE OUGHT to be a limousine: there's an old blue truck, with Mack in front and sheep behind. There's no matriarchy around – the women leave to trade themselves, the men – they don't know much, they're not yet lawyers, engineers. They hang about.

'Spying's the best,' Mack says to Ji. 'It's a knowledge job. It's not humanism, that would be quite out of place. It doesn't deal with futures, what happens to the *limes* – the limit we're all keen to reach, and not acknowledge. Spying's the plot that searches out the Plan, and tells the tale all round.'

Far above the moral threads, he thinks, the shifting carpet, the prayer rug they compose – there's the reality, the upper level where cruelty waves its sceptre, fingers its necklace – skull beads, bone spacers. The frigid lover, Adolphe, wins hands down; you're the fall guy. On to the next for both of you. Maybe you try another gamble, an accumulator, bet on some other partner, other horse, both keen to run.

There's still some sheep, safely they graze, the horses have been sold, the 'Jinghiz whites' go round and round in circuses.

'What's it about?' asks Mack. 'How do you know if you've done well or bad?'

'To do a history,' says Chagatai. 'You need comparisons. In a hundred years, we'll have an answer to your quiz,' and he and Ji laugh at Mack's bewilderment.

'Relax!' says Chagatai. 'We've some new sports, to test, amuse, the guests.'

He points to a tall tube. 'This is a centrifuge – it separates out the things you're made of ... it's between a curiosity and a diagnosis. You're spun, you turn into a kind of cheese – then, in reverse, it puts you back together, as you were, back into your clothes – reconstituted, all your solids, lymph and nameless curdish stuff... You could be analysed – an Emmenthal? Pecorino? Gorgonzola? It's for the young and bold. They make atom bombs with this, a model that has no reverse!... Then, there's the whirligig...'

And there's a cage, you perch within, it spins – 'Until you take no more!' Ji says. 'It's torture, but there's no response required – it's not to find out anything. It's just a sport – the centrifuge encloses you, it's dark; but in the whirligig, there's amusement in your expressions, your features spread and bloat, you weigh a ton, your eyes bulge out – you improvise the secrets that you haven't got, make promises you wouldn't keep.'

'And then,' Chagatai goes on. 'There is the Horse. We grew this from the bucking steed they have in bars – this one you ride and ride. You replicate the distances you had to cross when you were in a Horde – say, from here on to Moscow... It takes weeks.'

'I'm not sure these games are what I need,' says Mack.

'Oh, they're for guys who need a challenge, something that forces you beyond your nature, your everyday: makes you into something else...' says Chagatai. 'You swagger off, reborn.'

They stand awkward. Mack's no sport. 'They're all derived,' he says, 'from primal merrygorounds...'

'You pay to make a spectacle, that's all,' says Fulvio. 'Nothing is proved, and usually all turns back to what it was before. Your work, Mack, is more sophisticated. The spying covers everything: it's all an unknown realm, of course, no one is hurt, or stretched, or suffers vertigo... The games, instead – find out our limits: the spy investigates what's being done to push them back. Now, Mack – the dam you visited. That is a weapon. What's its point? That state's obsessed, its fear consumes. It has no enemy; the guys there threaten, but all want their isolation, independence. It's delicate ... maybe we could guarantee the dam won't break and flood ... or if it does ... we'll send them buckets... We have to make them feel secure...'

'I'm sure they'd like these games,' says Mack. 'An invitation? A free round?'

'Cash flow's a problem,' Fulvio says. 'There's always pushy capitalists – they want their money back, and more. More gambling – that is our salvation...'

'We'll ask Vivienne,' says Ji. 'She'll come and ride the Horse. We'll jiggle her until she yields. Forgives the debt.'

'You see,' says Chagatai. 'One super-horse is just a game, a sport. The real ones – they have disappeared. The surreal ones – well, with some cash, you'll make a million of them, riding West, South, East... Take some guys – like those in Anouk's prison: they can't be suppressed, nor roam around. Conscript them, train them up... They'll ride, ride to get away. This arid plain, though: it makes you weep...' and so he does.

'Grass,' says Ji. 'For us will always be inedible. Maybe another generation could digest. Fulvio could calculate those odds...'

'Of course,' says Chagatai, 'we have to think of Paco, mute and suffering down below. A remake! The Ten Commandments? That's a scenario for grown-ups ready-made. Ben Hur? A straight track, not the oval one. Bareback. A million horsemen on electric steeds – the charge – no mountains, rivers, in the way. The captives taken – into the whirligig! We keep our faith; there's no blood spilt riding in the tube. The centrifuge – put in reverse, the shape comes back, the bones stand up like osiers, the blood goes round and round again, like sitting ducks in shooting booths...'

'Listen, Chagatai,' says Mack. 'Nothing comes from nothing. A movie is not anything. You're all spied. Some dirty money may get through, unseen and unaccounted for. But all this crap – horses electric, Mongol lookalikes from reformatories – maybe a future looks like this. But it's not ours. It's all a movie scene. Remember a generation back; the battles with machines, wild, rusted out and glued together, guys in old nazi helmets, the biking set, warriors discharged and outlawed...'

'You're right,' of course,' says Ji. 'It's Paco territory. It's a remake. Conquest of the steppe, taking China, governing the sunshine lands. India. Russia – and the Middle. The culture – grandiose! True revolution. And yet, Mack, and yet... It's a fossil seed: an egg.'

'Those apocalypses,' Chagatai goes on, 'weren't a prefiguration, a foresight. Those movies embroidered, metaphorised what we know now: – warriors improvising on the sand: a disruptive creed, outlaws bunkered in encampments. It all came about...'

'It's not at all my reality,' Mack says. 'It's short term adventurism. "New small states..." not anarchy: Bakuninism, Ji. A macedonia of squabbling.'

'What you want,' says Ji. 'It always comes. Usually, you're not around. What you plan takes longer than you have to live. This place – is drying out. The animals have left, the rain holds back: the people flee. There's monks and us – we with a plan, and they without. They had one at the start – now they've forgotten it.'

'If you've a plan, Ji, it's "waiting for the wave",' says Mack.

'When you're at sea, that's what you do,' says Ji. 'One always comes along.'

'This is your holiday,' says Fulvio to Mack. 'We don't expect a sense from you. Saving the world, keeping advantages ... surviving, being the last ones ... that's your job, Mack, to see it all and pass it on. That's what everyone is watching here.'

'Money, Fulvio,' Mack says. 'It's a substance full of mystery. You had the money for this resort – cash fell like snow, up sprout these walls. Then – it all changed – rich people went to Memphis, the nature here dried up. Now, you've these new games... The world, Fulvio – you want to change the world with games! It isn't will, behind the change. It's luck ... all luck!'

'No, Mack,' Fulvio says. 'My speciality is *chance*. Luck is what *you* have – much more exciting. Chance is arithmetic, that keeps the money coming in. Luck is what makes you monk or waiter – or lets you run away. Or ride the Horse. Or take the train.'

'The train's bad luck for Mack,' says Ji, and laughs. 'Now – here's another point. We know about the famous Kalmuk, the most illustrious of all. Lenin! – his bowl-shaped skull, the yellow eyes ... a vision broad as Jinghiz had... Is that chance, what he engineered, or luck? Or something, maybe with a trace of both: you hear – he hears

– the rolling of the dice on baize, the eight-ball trundling on the slate ... perhaps a bet's involved, maybe just fishing for some luck...? No! It is the steppe, its call and flourish! Unbounded, no horizon, a green land full of woolly beasts...'

'You could live well here,' Mack says. 'This is the centre, that's for sure. But – it's precarious. You feel it teetering...'

'Better to choose relative poverty, than have absolute indigence thrust upon you,' says Chagatai. 'You fit in here, Mack. You should stay. Choose? You've no alternative, there is no other way. Everyone believes they have a choice – it isn't so. You always end up in your place. You've had your experiences, no great epiphanies. So, this is it, here you are, so let it carry you along – relax.'

'That's what Lily says,' says Mack. 'I've not reached a conclusion – so, "relax", she says.'

'Paco! Paco allots the part you need,' says Ji. 'His pictures have no corners, there's nowhere horror can hide away... That shirt he wears – it's made of flags, pink, orange, black and green – a walking prayer, the wind will lift him up to God. It's cheating, naturally. It's called post-production: those Japanese directors – they have armies bigger than he'll ever have ... but he's the master: his word, last, first, it's always his.'

*

Paco has aged. His face – a netsuke, an empty nutshell. The nose has fallen in, back to the monkey, the lips grimace – no teeth appear. The shirt – stops just above the testicles, two scorched dangling conkers. 'My friends,' he croaks, 'I am a mess!'

*

Like stars flung out – they've all done bad here: they are still stars, of course, but destined for a fiery 'ploff'! One last explosion, bang!, unnoticed in the dark, perhaps.

'No!' Mack says. 'I'm having an epiphany. The greatest movie won't be made. The gladstone with the cash – inflates, deflates... The cash, the notes, go obsolete... Poor Fulvio. Poor Chagatai, mine host forever at Reception – no one comes, and Ji – dreams on, the conquest, my! it's slow... He leads the charge – there's no one there, before, behind... Postponed: tomorrow, the great turnaround.

'Lily was right, I am relaxed. Only the monks have won – the trumpeting goes on, more flags flap up like flocks of doves – there's peace.'

'Too bad,' says Ji... 'You're wrong, Mack. You must be hard. The water disappears – the rocks remain, and more and more you see them, rising up...It toughens us, we are not finished – quite the reverse!'

10

MACK

'YOU'RE RELAXED?' asks Lily.

'Oh yes,' says Mack. 'Where I was – they're full of life. Planning things. They lift you up a tone. The contrary of what I am directed to – an altruistic decline. But – they're so full of life! Life in the broad sense – death included, Lily.'

'Your work's essential, Mack,' she says. 'How to survive with what there's left, how it can be done: the gain, the loss. Recovering from empires, Mack, that's just one part ... a heritage disordered.'

'Yes, yes,' says Mack. 'I was moved, terrified, dubious, when I was with them – Ji, Fulvio, and Chagatai. Poor Paco too, of course...'

'That's good,' says Lily. 'Good to be shaken up.'

'The thing is, Lily, all these guys – the bosses, bookies and the bankers – they say they're looking for a way we'll all survive. Eating grass is only part of it. But – when I say "we" – that too is only part of it,' says Mack. 'They want their country, or their enterprise, their group, religion, what knows what – to live and live. Subvert the others. When the rest go down – they'll rule: them and their gang – the *coqs de roche*... It might be regrettable, that all the rest have gone – but not a thing they'd mourn.'

'Of course,' says Lily. 'That is the point. Surviving means lots won't. Each hopes it will be them alive, and some or few along with them as well: otherwise, it's solitude. Robinson without the savage tribe. But never everyone. We're social, Mack, we do the math. If we were sheep or goats, we'd go ahead regardless, not recognise our peers, not count the grazers sharing grass. Us – we're species-conscious. We plot extinction's route. Making priorities – it's in our nature, our intelligence. We are the first: me, and sometimes you: second, or nowhere, all the rest.'

'My "sort of communism" then,' says Mack, 'is flawed. It's crap, as an idea, a goal.'

'The way you mean it, Mack, that's so,' says Lily, calling to Mirko. 'But – you're not a humanist. Those who're alive – not the others, lounging dumb in paradise...'

'They'll follow the priorities until there's only one of them remains,' says Mack. 'Robinson prefers a perfect solitude. A communism of one. The hungry Wolf, the frozen Adolphe ... they have their appetites ... my comrades will be gobbled up or dumped.'

'Don't be naive,' says Mirko. 'It won't happen. You'll be dead a while before.'

'Of course,' says Mack. 'The wrong guys rule – that's always so. You're right – continue in that sense, it shows how I'm naive, banal. When I saw Anouk again, I was entwined with her, her destiny. I should have given her boys, the prisoners, a boost instead. Give them the key, the code – kick in the backside that sets them into insurrection. The gunner's match, the powder trail.

'With Ji – I should have learned to ride, and twist the horse round like warriors do, getting off their shot.'

'Forget the archery,' says Lily. 'Spying – that's where your genius lies.'

'Odd,' says Mack. 'Fulvio said nothing of you being goodson to him, Mirko. Maybe you're not the only one...'

'Oh no,' says Mirko, 'it isn't that. It's just not done, to mention it.'

'Oh, you're soft, Mack,' Lily says, pinching both his cheeks and nestling, her nose at his nose. 'You're jello. That's why we love you so.'

'Keep on your path – you could be goodson to us both,' says Mirko, hugging Lily from behind.

'I'm not sure where it takes me, bonding so with both of you,' Mack says.

'It's natural, Mack, you want to be a hard, decisive type, like Ji,' says Lily, breaking herself free. 'It's best be what you are. In the end, you know, you will win out. You, Mack – you will be right!'

'Oh,' Mack says, 'I've given up some things – like wondering what's behind that iron door ...'

They laugh – and Lily says, 'Sort me out – those empires, lasting for centuries: Turks, Iranians and Mongols – even the Tibetans. But everyone talks about Americans – they made all those movies, covered history with them – they had high hopes, knew everything, then it fizzled out...'

'Oh Lily,' Mack says, 'you have to concentrate. It's names and places. I'll take you to those movies, if I must...'

'No, no,' says Mirko. 'There's too much work, not enough cash. Concentrate, Mack. Those guys left things as they were. Now, it's removing features counts, not removing frontiers, the *limes*, emirs and rajas. Now, there's new deserts, seas that disappear, the ice that melts. Mountains that crawl and slump.'

'Well,' Lily says, 'I hope Ji gets here. I can't wait to see the Horse.'

'Well, Lily, if they come – it will not be a movie, that's for sure. The whole land mass? Under Ji?' asks Mack, rhetorically. 'Our love, our wisdom and our song – where would those be?'

'Don't worry and don't mope,' says Lily, briskly. 'They've gone nowhere. They weren't yours. If you don't find other partners – it's your fault. Try to be attractive!'

'And don't speculate,' says Mirko, pushing Mack towards the stairs. 'Back to your prospect! Survival, that's the thing. Survival plus, of course – not grubs and roots, but maybe lamb with apricots!'

He laughs, he puts his hands on Lily's breasts. 'Up, up, dear Mack,' he shouts, as Mack goes up the tower.

ABOUT THE AUTHOR

John Fraser has lived in Rome since 1980. Previously, he worked in England and Canada.

www.ingramcontent.com/pod-product-compliance
Lightning Source LLC
Chambersburg PA
CBHW031331170626
46807CB00002B/652